Murder at Medicine Creek

A Tabitha Peterson Mystery

Lucy Glass

Lucy Glass, LLC

By Lucy Glass...

Tabitha Peterson Mystery Series:

Murder at Medicine Creek

Novella:

Arabesques and Alibis

About the Author

Lucy Glass is an author, musician, composer, and teacher. She's raised four children, three dogs, two cats, a horse, a rabbit, a ferret, and a rat named Vinnie, all with varying degrees of success.

She loves gallivanting around the world—in fact, her first story leaped into her head while sitting on the edge of a cliff in an Irish downpour while trying to catch her breath.

Lucy views life as a series of experiments and is a firm believer in trying, failing, then trying again. She blames it on her father, who completely forgot to teach her that there are things that just can't be done.

Lucy would love to connect with you at Lucy Glass Writes on Facebook, or say hello at hi@LucyGlassWrites.com. (She may even send you one of Gran's delicious cake recipes!)

Copyright © 2023 by Lucy Glass, LLC

All rights reserved.

No part of this publication may be reproduced, distributed, or transmitted in any form or by any means, including photocopying, recording, or other electronic or mechanical methods, without the prior written permission of the publisher, except as permitted by U.S. copyright law. For permission requests, contact Lucy Glass, LLC at hi@LucyGlassWrites.com.

The story, all names, characters, and incidents portrayed in this production are fictitious. No identification with actual persons (living or deceased), places, buildings, and products is intended or should be inferred.

Book Cover by JD Thompson

First edition 2023

To my children: Josh, Kati, Jake, and Hope

Who support me no matter what tomfoolery I get up to.

Contents

1. Death By Dryer — 1
2. Laundry Day — 8
3. Laundry Everywhere — 16
4. Six Weeks Earlier — 25
5. Music Appreciation — 35
6. Dinner At Gran's — 45
7. Office Visit — 51
8. Millie — 62
9. The Party — 74
10. New Year's Eve — 84
11. No. 2 — 92
12. First Day of School — 100
13. Pain All Around — 108

14.	Rumors	119
15.	Dead Composers	130
16.	The Hunt Is On	140
17.	The Plot Thickens	151
18.	Confrontations	163
19.	Closing In	172
20.	Sheep Pens	180
21.	Catsuits	189
22.	The Price To Pay	197
23.	Day Off	205
24.	Busted	214
25.	May Day	223
26.	Missing Persons	237
27.	All Tied Up	248
28.	In A Bow	254
New by Lucy Glass... Sweet Murder		265
Acknowledgements		267

Chapter 1

Death By Dryer

Tabitha Peterson rubbed her cheek against the still-damp towel in an attempt to push back the stray curl tickling it—a simple task for anyone *not* holding a gigantic laundry basket full of dirty clothes and detergent. A trickle of sweat rolled down her back. *Just up the hill*, the landlord said. *An easy walk*, she said. Tabitha's sweatpants were no match for this kind of cold. The sun shone weakly, warming her well enough when the front porch had blocked the wind, but now, without its protection, the gusts were bitter and fierce. She leaned over the basket, resting her chin on the clothes so they wouldn't blow away. *Hammerstein wasn't kidding.*

Several buildings clumped together as if for protection at the top of the hill. Some brick, some wood, some concrete, their facades giving the appearance of two stories, but from this angle it was clear they were not. She shifted the basket.

This is ridiculous. Who doesn't have a washer and dryer? My landlord, apparently.

Huge brown dead-looking bushes grew hodgepodge in the yard to Tabitha's right, and a gravel driveway led to an old house with peeling blue paint. An old floral couch sat crookedly on the front porch, as if it took every bit of the owner's energy to get it that far. The house had a neglected, if not outright abandoned feel. A tired-looking woman with a baby on her hip pushed open the battered screen door and waved.

"Howdy," she called from the rickety porch. Tabitha grinned widely, hoping that was good enough.

"You the new music teacher?" The woman, younger than Tabitha first thought, switched the child to her other hip and tugged a stained sweatshirt declaring *Don't Worry, Be Happy* down over her soft white belly.

Tabitha, surprised, nodded again. "Yes."

"Welcome to Medicine Creek. Good to meet ya." She twisted her head and yelled through the screen. "Rowdy, come out here." A young boy, maybe seven or eight, poked his head out. "This here's Rowdy. I guess you'll have him—and the little one here is Tanner. My oldest, Colt, is out at the barn with his father, but you won't have him. He's big into FFA."

"Hello, Rowdy. It's nice to meet you. I'm Ms. Peterson, your new music teacher." Rowdy saw no need to respond. "And you are...?" she asked his mother.

"Oh, sorry. I'm Stormy. Stormy Ryan." The baby started to fuss. "Well, I better git in and take care of this boy. I'm glad you're here. Rowdy didn't get on too good with the last teacher. Maybe he'll do better with you."

"I'll do my best. It's good to meet you."

The screen door rattled against its frame and Tabitha shifted the weight of the basket. *Why did I buy the giant laundry detergent? I'm an idiot. No I'm not. I didn't know I was going to have to walk uphill to a laundromat every week.* A pickup passed, its tires crunching as it turned into the gravel drive behind her. Someone cut the engine. Tabitha didn't look back, hoping to avoid more conversation. A screen door opened and banged shut. She breathed a sigh of relief, but a minute later the screen door creaked on its hinges again, the truck engine turned over, and an old truck—half red, half primer—pulled along beside her.

"You Ms. Peterson?"

Tabitha slapped on her best teacher smile. "Yes I am."

"Stormy said to give you a ride to the laundry mat. Git in." The man, thick and muscular, did not look friendly.

"Oh, I'm fine. It's not much farther." She waved him on as she walked, the truck creeping along beside her.

"I said git in."

"I don't want to be any trouble. Thank you, though. Have a good afternoon." She heard herself babbling but couldn't stop.

The truck pulled ahead, then stopped, and the man jumped out. He was short—he couldn't have been over five-foot-four or five—but still several inches taller than her. He took the laundry basket from her and lifted it into the bed of the truck.

"Git in," His voice, wooden and flat, mirrored his expression. He opened the passenger-side door. "Please," he added, his voice rusty, as if he didn't use it often.

Hmm. He's got my clothes and Stormy sent him. I'm sure it's fine. She scooted in, glad to get out of the wind.

He slammed the truck door, walked around the back of the truck, and climbed in.

"Thank you. My arms were aching. I appreciate it."

No response. It only took a few minutes to get to the laundromat and Tabitha didn't realize how bunched up her shoulders had been until they were standing in front of the building and he handed her the basket.

"Thank you."

He left without a word. *Weird. At least I didn't have to walk up the entire hill.*

Up close, the shops were as ramshackle as they appeared from the foot of the hill. The laundromat itself—a squat white concrete rectangle— had been painted white a long time ago, but years of Oklahoma wind and red dirt had turned it a pale, splotchy pink. *So this is my new home.*

Tabitha pushed the door open with her backside as heat and humidity blasted from inside, and she was grateful for the warmth. Against the wall was a motley group of old mismatched chairs, but someone had painted them bright colors, and it gave the laundromat a cheery, homemade feel. Tabitha breathed in the clean detergent and bleach smell. Today it was filled with women trying to get ahead of their weekend. A small boy and girl chased each other around a white folding table in the center of the room, the women dodging them as they carried laundry baskets from washer to dryer, dryer to folding table.

I can't imagine how busy this place must get on Saturdays. A young woman comforted a crying toddler as she took wet clothes from a washer. Tabitha glanced around the long, narrow room to see if anyone was waiting for it, but it seemed like everyone was more interested in the dryers. *I'm glad I didn't come earlier.* She set the basket on the floor and measured the detergent, threw in her bedding and towels, then popped in her earbuds to avoid making small talk. All the chairs were taken so she sat in the window seat. It seemed to Tabitha that everyone was old friends, or at least knew each other. A few women smiled at Tabitha. She nodded and smiled back, but it felt awkward and she pulled out her phone. She'd sworn to herself she was never playing *Candy Crush* again but now was glad she hadn't deleted it. Another washer opened up and Tabitha filled it with delicates. The place was thinning out now. By the time her second load finished, she was alone but for an older woman, although several dryers were still running.

"I guess this town is safe, if people leave their clothes unattended?"

"They aren't unattended. I'm here," the woman answered. She narrowed her eyes. "You thinking of stealin' something?"

"No! " Tabitha said, alarmed. "No. Do we have to wait to use a dryer until someone comes for their laundry?"

"No. Just take 'em out. But fold 'em. Don't just throw 'em around."

"Of course, of course." Tabitha tapped her foot. *I do not want to be trapped here chatting with this old woman.* She paced the length of the laundromat and spied a dryer in the far corner not in use. "Why isn't anyone using this one?" she asked, pointing.

"There should be a sign on it. It doesn't get hot. Fluff and cool is all that works."

Tabitha wandered over. An old piece of masking tape clung to the glass door. She spied a corner of paper under the dryer and plucked it from the concrete floor. The words *No Heat* were scrawled in red crayon on the paper torn from a spiral notebook. "There's stuff in it."

The woman shrugged. "Try it. Maybe it's fixed."

Tabitha unloaded the washers, carried the wet, heavy load to the end of the room, and pulled on the dryer door, but it didn't budge. She set the basket down and tugged hard with both hands. It popped open, and Tabitha stepped back, her hands flying to her chest.

"Oh my god."

"We don't say that around here." The woman glanced over to see Tabitha riveted on the content of the dryer, mouth gaping, green eyes wide. She hurried over and peeked inside. Stuffed inside was a tiny man, his rump facing them.

"Who's that?" she demanded, looking at Tabitha like she would know. Tabitha could only shake her head, her hand now over her mouth. The woman poked at him with one bony finger. Nothing. She closed the door and inserted a quarter.

"What are you doing?" Tabitha said, shocked.

"I couldn't get a good look at him." She bent over, eyes scrunched up, nose to the dryer window while the drum rotated, then straightened and opened the door. A shock of fluffy gray hair flopped over a pair of large, inquisitive, glassy blue eyes.

He looks surprised to see us. The woman turned to Tabitha, hands on her bony hips, and blinked once.

"What is Vinnie the Rat doin' in the dryer?"

Chapter 2

Laundry Day

The old lady grabbed Vinnie's arm and pulled hard. She couldn't have weighed ninety pounds. "Boy, is he wedged in there. Grab his arm and help me."

Tabitha jerked her head back, wild-eyed. "I'm not touching him!"

"Do you know some other way to get him out? Don't be a baby." She hiked a scrawny leg, wedged a hot pink Converse up against the dryer for leverage, and gave the arm another good tug. "Nope. This is a two-woman job."

"Well, I'm not doing it. We should call the police."

"That's a good idea. Call the police."

Tabitha pulled her phone from her back pocket. *Two percent. Why did I play Candy Crush? Maybe I can still make the call.*

"What's the number?"

"Number to what?"

"The police. What's the number?"

"I don't know. Goggle it."

Gogg—? Oh. *Google* it. You said 'goggle'."

"No I didn't."

Tabitha sighed. It was like talking to a seven-year-old. She began to punch in the number, then stopped and put the phone in her pocket.

"Why aren't you typing? You gotta get the phone number," said the woman.

"I can't. It's dead. Is there a landline in here?

"Nope."

"Do you know where the police station is?"

"We don't have one."

"No police station?"

"Nope."

"Then why did you tell me to call the police station?"

"That was your idea. Myself, well, I'd go over to the sheriff's office."

"The sheriff's office. Do you know where the sheriff's office is?"

"Sure, I do. I've lived here my whole life."

Tabitha sucked in air. *I can't shake a little old lady.* "Do you have a car?"

"Nope."

Tabitha closed her eyes. *Think.* "Okay. Give me directions to the sheriff's office. I'll run."

"You're gonna run to the sheriff's office?"

"Oh my god, just tell me how to get there."

"You know, we don't—"

Tabitha's right eyebrow shot up.

"Fine. Go out the door and turn right."

Tabitha blew out air, beyond exasperated. "And then...?"

The woman narrowed her eyes as she evaluated Tabitha, then spoke again, enunciating each syllable. "And-then-tell-them-Vinnie-is-stuck-in-the-dryer." The two women glared at each other, each wondering about the other's sanity. "And see if you can get Atticus to come. He's strong. I bet he can get him out."

"Where. Is. The. *Sheriff's* office?"

"Don't get testy." She jutted an arthritic thumb to her right. "Like I said, go outside and turn right. It's next door."

....

Medicine Creek Sheriff's Department, painted in gold, adorned the heavy glass door, and the wind made it nearly impossible to open. Tabitha had to use both hands and once she finally tugged it open, she struggled to close it.

"Hurry up. You're freezing me out." A big woman in bright pink lipstick and matching sweater sat at the front desk. A nameplate with *Deputy Bird* emblazoned in gold sat neatly centered, a jar of jellybeans to her left. "I guess the front is moving in."

"I need to speak with Deputy Bird, please."

"That's me."

The woman caught Tabitha's gaze flitting to the pink sweater encasing her massive bosom. "I'm not exactly built for a uniform."

Tabitha shook her head, momentarily distracted. "I'd like to report a crime."

The deputy looked at her blankly.

Tabitha tried again. "I'm Tabitha Peterson. A crime has been committed."

"You new in town?"

"Yes, I'm the new music teacher, and there's been a —"

"Atticus, come meet the new music teacher," the woman yelled over her shoulder.

A door in the back creaked open and a tall, muscular cowboy ambled in. "So you're the music teacher. Welcome to Medicine Creek. To what do we owe the honor?"

It took Tabitha a second to remember why she was there. "I need to report a crime," she said for the third time.

"Okay. What crime are you reporting?" His smile, disarmingly lopsided, temporarily distracted Tabitha. *The old lady at the laundromat is right; you do look strong.*

"I was washing my clothes and needed to dry them and my phone died and this old lady tried to pull him out—" Tabitha's eyes filled and she grabbed the back of a chair, dizzy.

"Whoa. Slow down and take a breath." He sauntered over and stood closer than was strictly necessary, which didn't help matters. She looked up at him and took a deep breath. He smelled good.

"Better?" Her head bobbed up and down. "Good. So tell me what's going on."

"Vinnie's stuck in the dryer."

··········

Atticus stood in front of the dryer, arms folded across his chest, the lop-sided smile gone.

"You didn't mention that Vinnie was dead." He made a call, all business now. "Did you touch anything?"

"No. Yes," the two women said in unison.

"Aunt Agnes, what did you touch?"

Aunt Agnes? These two are related? Tabitha rubbed her temples.

"Well, I always do my wash on Fridays. Before the rush, you know—"

Atticus interrupted. "Aunt Agnes."

"Yeah, yeah, I know. Focus." She tapped her fingertips together. "Okay. I touched the dryer door. So did she." Agnes pointed at Tabitha like this was all her fault.

"So I'll find both your prints on the handle. Is that all?"

"My Nike touched the front of the dryer, so if you find a shoe print in a size five, that's me, but I swear, I did not stuff Vinnie in the dryer."

Atticus cut his eyes to Tabitha. *Did the corner of his mouth just twitch?*

"I don't suppose either of you saw Vinnie get in the dryer. Did you see him come in? Anything unusual at all?" The women shook their heads.

A bell tied on the front door jingled as Yaeleen and a small, thin, middle-aged man entered. Atticus waved them to the back of the laundry.

"Doc, thank you for getting here so fast. The body is over here. Aunt Agnes, would you go to the office and make a list of everyone you saw here today?"

"You betcha', but what about my laundry? My lucky orange pant-suit is in the dryer."

"You can get it after we've processed the crime scene. Yaeleen will give you a call when we're through."

"Okey dokey." Aunt Agnes trotted off, the importance of her mission written all over her face.

Atticus turned his attention to Tabitha. "Do you have anything to add?" Tabitha shook her head from side to side. "Then I guess you can go, too. I'm sorry this is your first glimpse of our little town. It's usually peaceful around here." Tabitha had the laundromat door open when he called her name. "Miss Peterson?"

Tabitha braced herself as a gust of Oklahoma wind almost whipped the door out of her hand. The clip she'd used to pile her hair on top of her head finally gave up and auburn curls blew everywhere. She attempted to corral them to no avail. She gave up and waited for the sheriff to continue. *You're cute, in a cowboy sort of way.*

"May I have your number?"

Tabitha blushed. "I'm sorry, but I'm married." She noted the look on his face and hurried on. "Well, newly divorced, but I'm not ready to date yet." That lopsided grin again. *Okay, more than cute.*

"I'm flattered, but I need a contact number for the investigation."

Tabitha's cheeks flamed. "Of course. I'm, ah... It's..." A tear trickled down her cheek, and she could feel her face threaten to crumble. *I will not fall apart in front of this man.* She could not remember her phone number for the life of her. Her lip quivered.

"I'm staying at Mrs. Lovejoy's place for now," she said, then dashed out the door. Atticus watched her hurry down the sidewalk before turning to the task at hand—how to extract Vinnie from the dryer.

Chapter 3

Laundry Everywhere

The Lovejoy house sat in the center of what had been an old farmstead. Every few years it received a new coat of sunny yellow paint, and the gleaming white porch railing stretching the length of the house completed its cheerful look. Several mismatched rocking chairs provided seating for the home's occupants and guests, and a hand-made wind chime tinkled softly in the breeze. A metal stairway had been added to the outside of the house when the attic was converted into apartments a few years ago, but Tabitha hadn't yet received a key, so climbed the porch steps and entered through the front door. Inside, a wide stairway separated the dining room on the left from the living room on the right. Behind the dining room was a big country kitchen and pantry. Mrs. Lovejoy's bedroom nestled behind the warm, inviting living room.

The house, while it had seen better times, gleamed, and Tabitha found it charming inside and out. Mrs. Lovejoy had seen no need for updates, and it made Tabitha happy for a reason she couldn't articulate. She had assumed she'd be able to find a nice apartment with no trouble, but nice apartments were not to be found in Medicine Creek, although a decrepit old hotel advertising long-term stays lurked on the outskirts of town. She'd already heard what the locals called it: *The Hoe'-tel.* And it was no place for a school teacher, the principal had assured her. He gave her the name of a respected older woman who might have an apartment available. She had, and Mrs. Lovejoy welcomed Tabitha with open arms. It turned out to be more of a room than an apartment and shared a Jack-and-Jill bathroom with the occupant on the other side, but it was large and airy, and close enough to the school to walk. Tabitha had no kitchen, but meals were included in the rent, which meant she wouldn't have to cook. It would work for now at least.

She'd cried off and on during her walk back, and with the wind blowing dust everywhere, muddy rivulets now streaked her cheeks. Tabitha hoped she could get upstairs without seeing her new landlord. She opened the heavy Craftsman door as quietly as she could and almost made it to her room before Mrs. Lovejoy called to her from the kitchen.

"Is that you, Tabitha?"

"Yes. I'm just going to my room." Tabitha heard a pot clanging.

"I found the key to the outside door. Hang on, and I'll bring it to you."

"Don't trouble yourself. I'll get it later."

"No trouble at all." Mrs. Lovejoy rounded the corner. Her black hair, sprinkled with gray and clipped short, gave her a no-nonsense look. Tabitha guessed she was around sixty years old. "We're having dinner at six, and I always fix a nice dessert on Fridays. Oh, and my boy's back so you'll get to meet him. " She fished around in her pocket for the key but stopped, alarmed, when she noticed Tabitha's red eyes and tear-stained face.

"What happened, dear?" Her obvious concern brought on a new round of tears.

"There was an incident at the laundry. It was... it was..." She closed her eyes and took a deep breath before continuing.

"Let me stop you right there. A cup of hot tea is what you need. Go wash your face and lie down. This town is small and word gets around fast. I'm sure I'll find out soon enough. Go on upstairs and I'll bring that tea."

Tabitha nodded, grateful she didn't have to talk about it. She washed her face and felt somewhat better. Once in her room, however, she saw the bare mattress, remembered her bedding still at the laundromat, and dissolved into tears again. Mrs.

Lovejoy tapped twice on the door, then entered without waiting for an answer. She set the tea tray on the small table under the window and patted Tabitha's shoulder without saying a word, then left but returned immediately with a set of fluffy white bath towels and a bathrobe.

"A hot shower always makes me feel better. Your tea will be steeped by the time you finish. I better start dinner."

"Thank you. It's very kind of you." Tabitha pulled her phone out once the door closed. A sage green over-stuffed armchair with a white cotton throw folded across the back was placed near the window, and Tabitha sat down, exhausted, and plugged the phone into the charger. She began to punch in her mother's number, then stopped halfway. She knew what her mother would say and didn't want to hear it, and besides, it would only scare her.

Who could I call? Zamarri. Zamarri always laughs and makes me feel better. But I'm not ready to laugh about this just yet. I need to process everything. I'll call Nita—the voice of reason.

"You've reached Nita Crawford. Please leave a message."

"It's Tabitha. Give me a call."

She flopped back in the chair and scrolled through her favorites list. Michael's name was still at the top. *Michael. He's the last person I should talk to about this.* She tapped in his number. His phone rang several times. *This is crazy.* She started to hang up when he answered.

"Hello, Tabs."

She closed her eyes at the use of the hated nickname. "Hi."

"How are you doing?"

"Fine." *Fine? I'm anything but fine.*

"What's up?"

She didn't respond right away. *What in the world do I say—I found a dead man in the dryer?*

"Tabitha? Hello? You there?"

"I'm here."

"So... why'd you call?"

She burst into tears. She heard him sigh.

"Tabby. You've got to let me go."

You think that's why I called?

"I found a dead man in the dryer." *Oh my god, I said it. Why did I say that?*

"What?"

"I found a body in the dryer at the laundromat."

"You were at a laundromat? Where the hell *are* you?"

"Medicine Creek. It doesn't matter where I am."

"You actually took that job in the middle of nowhere? Tabs, you're a city girl. What were you thinking?"

"I love it here." She rolled her eyes at the lie.

"Why didn't you stay in the city?"

You jerk. "Because you divorced me and kicked me out of my home. Oh, and by the way—you didn't file the papers yet, did you?"

Michael ignored her. "I can't believe—no, of course I can. You could have moved in with your mother, but, as always, you jumped into something without thinking it through."

Like marrying you. Tabitha massaged her temples. *This is certainly not helping my headache.*

He continued. "So you're upset because you had to go to a laundromat and you want me to feel sorry for you."

"I'm upset because I found a man *dead* at the laundromat. I'm hanging up."

·····•····

Mrs. Lovejoy was right, I do feel better. The bathrobe dwarfed her but felt warm and cozy and smelled like sunshine. Tabitha didn't have the energy to dry her hair so just twisted it and used a clip again. She opened the bathroom door to find a soft blue chenille bedspread on her bed, turned back to reveal white cotton sheets covered in tiny blue and lavender flowers. It was nothing like her perfect, minimalist apartment, but somehow felt just right. Comforting. *Mrs. Lovejoy is such a dear,* she thought as she snuggled under the covers and drifted off.

She slept for a couple of hours before a tap on her door woke her.

"I hate to wake you, dear, but dinner will be ready soon."

Groggy, Tabitha merely nodded. She stretched and sat up as memories of the day flooded in. A door slammed downstairs and loud voices drifted up from the front lawn. Tabitha looked out the window to see flashing lights. She threw on a pair of jeans and a tee shirt and ran down the stairs barefoot. The front door was ajar, and she could see the sheriff's Ranger parked at the curb. In the middle of the yard stood Atticus holding her laundry basket, engrossed in conversation with someone she couldn't see, and he did not look pleased.

Just as she reached the front porch, a strong gust of wind blew her laundry from the basket, distributing most of it across the lawn. Tabitha watched, horrified, as her undies tumbled across the grass. She rushed down the front steps to retrieve them without noticing the tall, dark-haired man standing on the far side of the porch. Atticus shoved the basket into her arms and scrambled after the clothes.

"I am so sorry," he shouted over the wind. "Don't worry, I'll get them."

Tabitha stood by helplessly as Atticus ran around the yard gathering her unmentionables. *Can it get any worse?* From the corner of her eye, she saw the man on the porch lean over the railing to pluck a pair of pink panties off a rose bush. *Why, yes it can.* She had no idea who this strange, dark man could be, but here he was, holding her underwear out to her.

"Thank you," she said, trying not to look up, and failing. He seemed even taller up close.

"You are welcome." His skin was burnished, his cheekbones high, and his eyes dark and hooded as he studied her. His face showed no emotion and she had to look away. It felt as if he was invading her space, although he had done nothing of the sort and she knew it. She looked at Atticus to find him staring at her also, his arms full of clothes. *This is too much. Where do I look?* she asked herself wildly.

Atticus stuffed the clothes back in the basket.

"We need to talk," he said.

"We do?" It sounded stupid even as she said it.

"Yes. May I come in?"

"This is not a good time," the stranger said. Tabitha looked at him, surprised. "She has been through enough today. We are about to have dinner, then she needs to rest. Your questions can wait until tomorrow."

"I'm afraid they can't." Atticus was tall, but not as tall as this man. Atticus was muscular and built like a bull, while the other man looked lean, agile, and strong. The malice between the two men was palpable.

Tabitha saw how their muscles tensed, and realized that one wrong move could start something ugly. *These are dangerous men.* She felt lightheaded at the thought.

Atticus stared hard at the man before addressing Tabitha again. "We can talk here or I can take you to the sheriff's office—whichever suits you."

Tabitha hadn't noticed Mrs. Lovejoy come out.

"Atticus Blackhorn, this girl has had a day. She's going to come in and eat her dinner before it gets cold. I'll send her in the morning. Now go home."

Atticus sighed as he took his hat off and wiped his brow. "Gran, I need to talk to her now. There's been a murder."

"I know that. But he's not coming back to life whether you talk to her tonight or tomorrow, and this girl has had enough. I say it can wait. Nick, get her basket and you two come eat. We'll see you in the morning, Atticus. Tell your mother I said hi."

Atticus knew when he was beat. "Will do, Gran. Just have her there first thing, okay?"

The tall man took the laundry basket and herded Tabitha inside. *Who is this man? Is it too much to ask for a calm, quiet place to heal and start over?* When she'd found the advertisement for a music teacher in a small, sleepy town, she thought Medicine Creek would be perfect, but now she wondered. *What have I gotten myself into?*

Chapter 4
Six Weeks Earlier

"Tabby. Baby. Are you sure you're not biting off more than you can chew?" Michael pulled her closer and kissed the top of her head, then curled a strand of her hair around his finger. Tabitha took her feet off the sofa table and sat up. He smiled indulgently, which made her madder.

"You don't think I can do it," she said, tearing up despite herself.

"It's not that I think you can't do it. I know you're a smart girl—"

"I'm thirty-six years old."

He rolled his eyes. "Okay, you're a smart *woman*. But I know how much you like to start things—" That smile again. "Not so good at finishing, though."

Tabitha felt the familiar heat creep into her cheeks as her eyes welled, determined not to let the tears spill over.

"Ah, honey. Don't cry. I don't even know why you would put yourself through another audition. You're all nerves beforehand, then mope around afterward. And it's not like you have extra time."

"I am a classical musician."

"Of course you are. You have your quartet."

"That's for fun. It's not a real gig."

"Well, you could always play at church."

"We don't go to church."

"We could start." He grinned, unable to keep a straight face. Tabitha doubted he'd ever been to church in his life.

"Look, I'm late. Sure you don't want to go with me?" He grabbed his racket and jacket.

"You know I don't do sports."

"Suit yourself. But don't complain to me about your weight when you won't do anything about it."

She knew the pink spots were still there.

"Why don't you call your mother? Maybe she'll have some good advice. She's happy."

Tabitha's lips drew up into what Nita called her teacher smile. "Good idea. I'll see you later."

Michael poked his head around the front door. "Oh, and Tabby?"

My name is Tabitha. "Yes?"

"All my white tee shirts are dirty. And maybe you could go to the grocery store and make something healthy for dinner since you're not doing anything?"

"Absolutely." Her smile was dazzling. "Have a good time."

"You, too."

··········

"Hello?" Polly Peterson bubbled as she answered the phone.

Michael's right; how could my mother sound so happy just answering the phone?

"Hi, Mom. What are you doing?"

"Talking to my favorite daughter. What are you doing?"

"Not much. I'm making a run to the grocery store, but thought I'd give you a call first." Tabitha googled *fast healthy dinners*. "So Mom... got any plans? Want to meet for coffee?"

"I would, but I've got water aerobics."

"Ah."

"Why don't you go with me? It's a fun group."

Tabitha rolled her eyes. *Why does everyone want me to exercise? Besides, Mom, the median age is somewhere around seventy.*

"No thanks. I've got to practice."

"Oh, that's nice. What are you practicing for? Are you playing somewhere?"

Tabitha sighed. "No. No I'm not."

"Then why are you practicing?"

"So I'll get better, Mom!"

Her mother took a moment to digest this information. "Music is such a nice hobby."

Tabitha closed her eyes. "It's not a hobby. I have a master's degree in music performance."

"Yes, honey, I know. I'm glad you have something to keep you busy. I need to go. Can't be late for class. Love you."

"I love you, too, Mom. Have a good time."

Tabitha dialed Nita's number.

"You've reached Nita Crawford. Please leave a message."

"Hey, Nita. Call me. My life is falling apart. As usual. Please call before I murder everyone I love."

She scrolled through the recipes. *Tofu on cabbage*. That ought to fix him.

··········

Her phone rang just as the cashier leaned through the Wok-N-Roll drive-through window with her egg rolls.

"Hey, sorry I missed you. What's up?" Nita asked.

"Nothing new. My family is a constant reminder that my life sucks." Tabitha dug through the bag and pulled out an egg roll.

"Spill." Nita was nothing if not succinct.

"Michael doesn't want me to audition."

"I'm confused. Is Michael your father?"

Tabitha rolled her eyes as she took a bite of the egg roll. *Hot, hot, hot.* She breathed through her mouth, trying to keep the hot, oily cabbage from burning the roof of her mouth. *I hope Nita can't hear me chew through the speakerphone.*

"No, Nita. Michael is not my father. You know that."

"You can understand my confusion. I know he's not your boss because I am your boss. You do know he's not your boss?"

"Yes, I do. But it's complicated."

"I disagree, but let's move on. Who else are you murdering? Is your mother on your hit list?"

Tabitha laughed and almost choked on her egg roll. She grabbed the warm bottle of water that had been in her cup holder since Friday. "You know me too well. She called my music a hobby."

"Have you gone pro and didn't tell me?"

"No," Tabitha said, exasperated.

"Then, technically, your mother is correct. Take her off your list."

"Nita, you're supposed to be on my side. Give me advice. Tell me what to do."

"I am on your side, and I tell you exactly what to do. Just imagine what your life would be like if you were in charge." The car in front hit its brakes and Tabitha swerved hard to avoid it.

"Haha. It's not that easy."

"Of course it's not. Letting other people run your life is easy. And by the way, how's that working out?"

"Nita, I called so you could make me feel better."

"Hmm. So now I'm in charge of how you feel? The burden is heavy."

"I'm hanging up. You've been no help at all."

"Yes, I have. I've shared my wisdom, which is better than advice."

"Oh, brother."

"One more thing, before you hang up. If you must kill someone, I vote for Michael, but leave your mother alone. I like her. She brings me cookies."

··········

Tabitha pulled into the driveway and shut off the engine. She grabbed the grocery bags from the passenger seat and juggled them on her hip as she wrangled the key in the front door. She kicked it shut behind her, then stood in the entry to the kitchen, surveying the scene. It was just as she'd left it. *If Brownies were only real...* Two days' worth of dishes sat in the sink, and two more days' worth on the counter. She set the grocery bags on a chair and piled more dirty dishes in the sink, then glanced at the oven clock. Michael wouldn't be home for another couple of hours; more than enough time to wash his tee shirts, load the dishwasher, and still have a healthy meal on the table. Her phone rang and she pulled it out of her back pocket.

"Hey, Zamarri!" Holding the phone against her shoulder, Tabitha opened the refrigerator door and stuffed the grocery bags inside without bothering to unpack them.

"Hello, darling. Are you practicing right now? I hope I didn't disturb you."

"No, I just got home. I can talk."

"Wonderful. I've heard gossip about the audition. The two players from Germany have both dropped out. They were your real competition. I think you will easily win the audition."

"I hope so," said Tabitha, fishing through a drawer to find a clean dishrag.

"No. Do not hope. Do not wish. Hoping and wishing are for children. Work. You know this. Your work ethic at university inspired everyone." Zamarri waited for a response. Nothing. "Tabitha, you are practicing, aren't you? You are focused?"

"Of course," Tabitha said, her voice flat.

"If you win, think how much fun we'll have together. Rumor is, we're going to Budapest in the fall. And you'll be able to quit your teaching job." Tabitha searched under the sink for dish soap. "Tabitha? Are you there?"

"Yes." Tabitha could hear Zamarri sigh.

"I begin to think I want this for you more than you. I have to run. Rehearsal, you know. Go practice. We'll talk soon."

Tabitha looked at the dirty dishes stacked in the sink, suddenly exhausted. She walked into the bedroom with every intention of gathering Michael's tee shirts, but instead flopped on the bed and stared at the ceiling.

What am I going to do? I would have already gone pro if I hadn't married Michael.

She pulled her phone from her pocket to call—*Who? Pull yourself together, girl. I love Michael. I love being married. I have good friends at work. Everything will be fine. I am fine.*

Tabitha jumped off the bed, took a quick shower, threw the laundry in the washer, and started dinner. Michael would be home soon. She'd practice extra hard tomorrow.

·········

"Aren't you eating?" Michael asked between bites.

"I had a few bites. I'm trying to cut back," said Tabitha, full of egg rolls.

Michael pushed his plate away. "You know, I don't think I'm a big fan of tofu."

Tabitha grinned to herself. *I didn't think you would be.* She reached over to take his plate. Michael caught her hand and pulled her into his lap.

"You know I love you, don't you?"

"Mm-hmm," she said, wondering what he was up to.

He tilted her head and kissed her cheek. "Why don't you go practice and I'll do the dishes."

Tabitha stroked the carefully manicured stubble on his cheek. "That is so sweet. I appreciate it. This day's been a little rough. If I could play for a couple of hours that would be amazing."

"Hey, Tabby, guess what I'd like to play…"

She grinned, the dishes forgotten.

Thirty minutes later she stretched and kissed his back, content. "I think I'll go practice now. I'm feeling inspired," she whispered. No response. Tabitha rolled onto her back and examined the ceiling, feeling her contentment dissipate, then pushed herself onto her knees to peek over his shoulder. Michael snored lightly. *Of course.* She hopped out of bed and walked into the bathroom to shower.

Michael opened the bathroom door as she stepped out. "You know," he said, rubbing his eyes. "You're a beautiful woman."

Tabitha blushed. "Thank you."

He made a grab for her towel, but she stepped back and snatched it before he could. "I'm thinking what you'd look like if you worked out."

She wondered if he was capable of complimenting her without ruining it. "Close the door. I'm freezing."

"Come back to bed." She mentally rolled her eyes, his sexy grin lost on her.

"No. I'm practicing and you're doing the dishes, remember?"

"Yeah, but now I'm all relaxed." He tried to pull her close but she dodged him and went into the bedroom.

She heard him lift the toilet seat. "So you aren't going to do the dishes?"

"Tabs," he said over his shoulder, "don't spoil the mood. Come back to bed."

"It's practice time. Like we agreed," she added, pulling on a tee and sweatpants.

She could hear the flush, then frowned as he flopped onto the bed face down.

"Suit yourself." He lifted his head. "But keep it down, okay?"

Chapter 5
Music Appreciation

"Michael, I'm going to work. See you tonight," Tabitha called out as she closed the front door. She threw her backpack in the passenger seat and turned the key, flinching as Metallica blasted from the radio. She turned down the volume and flipped it to NPR, glad she left for work before Michael got up, then immediately felt guilty, but only a little. The commute to school also guaranteed some alone time, and she enjoyed her morning routine.

She pulled into the gas station and ran inside to grab a coffee and banana. A short line of regulars waited to get their morning fix.

"Hey, girl," the check-out clerk yelled. Tabitha glanced over her shoulder. Today the clerk's hair boasted neon pink and green hues.

"Hey, Starr. Looking good."

The homeless man ahead of her turned at the sound of Tabitha's voice.

"Hey, Ray," she said.

"Good morning. I missed you yesterday." He smiled and she counted three teeth.

"Yesterday was Sunday. I was home."

"Home is good," he said. She wanted to say home might be over-rated, but considering his circumstances, thought better of it. At the counter, she flapped her hand in Ray's direction.

"I've got his coffee, and tell him to get a banana."

Starr nodded. "Will do. You're a good person."

Tabitha shrugged. "It's just a coffee and banana. See you tomorrow."

·····•····

The School of Performing Arts, a squat building made of cinder block, sat on a large lot in the heart of the city. Although not much to look at from the street, once inside, its gleaming blue and green tiles emanated a quiet joy—at least for Tabitha. She smiled, listening to a few students warming up in practice rooms. She took a sip of coffee as she walked down the hall. The door to the ballet studio stood open and Tabitha poked her head in.

Miki, already in the zone, hummed as she danced. Tabitha leaned against the wall, watching, not wanting to disturb her.

Once satisfied, Miki marked the steps on a clipboard resting on top of a grand piano before waving Tabitha over.

"New choreography?"

"For the Spring Gala."

"Already? It's just the second week in November." *And I'm not even finished working on the Winter Showcase.* "It looks great so I assume it's going well?"

Miki stretched out her calves at the barre. "So far. I found a wonderful piano piece by Andre Previn. I want a piano on stage with the dancers. Very minimalist." She wiped the sweat from her chest with the hand towel she kept at the end of the barre. "How are you?"

"Good. I got a new student this semester. She has some bad habits, but she's sweet and eager to learn. But I think her father's military, so who knows how long she'll be here."

"How's Carly?"

"Carly's been accepted to Julliard, so she's on top of the world. I'm excited for her. She'll do well; she's a brilliant student. I'll miss her." Tabitha downed the last of her coffee. "I'll see you at lunch. Have a good day."

··········

She had the key to her studio in her hand when Nita rounded the corner.

"Tabitha. Just the person I wanted to see."

"What's up, Nita?" Tabitha asked, unlocking the door.

"You're not going to like this."

Tabitha turned on the light and dropped her empty coffee cup in the trash can.

"Hmm."

"Oliver Pressman just quit."

"The new orchestra conductor? Well, that didn't take long. Why is he leaving?"

Nita shrugged. "He got offered a chance to conduct in Boston and he took it."

"But he can't leave in the middle of the year unless you release from him his contract, right?"

"Of course I released him. I would never be responsible for anyone missing such a great opportunity. I'm not cruel." Nita studied a plaster bust of Mozart. "Do you think he looked like that?"

"Can't say that I know. Have you found a replacement?"

"Yes, but there's a catch. You know Oliver taught a few other classes."

"Theory and Composition."

"Yes. And Music Appreciation."

"Ugh."

"The new guy can start in a week. Matthew Barry. He just finished his studies in France. He's young, but he's good."

"Great! So what's the catch?"

"He refuses to teach Music Appreciation."

Tabitha laughed. "I don't blame him. That class should be banned."

"So I am hoping you will teach it." Nita set the bust down and picked up a large piece of quartz. "Pretty."

"Wait. Why me?"

"Because you are the newest teacher in the department." She grinned. "And everyone else already refused."

Tabitha made a face as she set her backpack in the corner. "Sure, I'll do it. It'll be fun."

"I knew I could count on you."

At lunch, Tabitha sent Zamarri a quick text:

> Are you saying putting others first is irresponsible?

> I did not. Hope you learn to love Music Appreciation. It looks like you may be teaching it for a long time

> You don't have anyone to think about but yourself. I'm married; I don't have that luxury

Tabitha turned her phone to silent. *I don't need your judgment, Zamarri. I live in the real world.* She looked around the cafeteria and sighed. *Is Zamarri right? Am I sabotaging my life?* Tears threatened to well up. *Zamarri's blunt, but I was snarky. She didn't deserve that.* She texted an apology and wiped her eyes as Miki floated in and opened her lunch box. Her meal, like Miki herself, was a mystery to Tabitha. Although they were the same height, Miki was several sizes smaller. People tended to use words like delicate and ethereal to describe Miki. Tabitha was just short. She remembered her mother describing her as sturdy once. Miki ate almost nothing. Her lunch box, always stuffed to the brim, contained mostly celery and greens with the occasional strawberries or a few nuts. Tabitha never seemed to have time to pack a lunch. Today's cafeteria menu proclaimed loaded baked potatoes, which she secretly looked forward to.

"Miki, did you do anything fun this weekend?"

"Hero and I flew to Boston for the opening of Tosca–it's one of his favorite operas—then we met some old friends for Sunday brunch. There is a new art exhibit at the Museum of Fine Arts, so we made a quick detour on the way to the airport. What did you do?"

"Michael's laundry," Tabitha said under her breath.

"I'm sorry, I didn't catch that. What?"

"Nothing. We Just hung around the house."

"Well, it's good to just relax every now and then," she said, munching her way delicately through her celery and carrots. Tabitha nibbled at her baked potato, feeling guilty. Her eyes followed Miki's. She'd dribbled melted cheese onto her shirt. She picked up her brown cafeteria napkin and smeared it further. Miki had been a principal dancer in London—and Tabitha couldn't manage to get a fork full of food from her tray to her mouth without making a mess.

"Once we stayed home the entire weekend." Miki dabbed at the corner of her mouth with her pinky.

"All three days?" *Miki, deep in my heart I am rolling my eyes.*

"Yes." Miki's laugh sounded like little silver bells. "I thought I would climb the walls. I mean, who does that?"

"Yeah, who?" Tabitha pushed her chair back, dumped her tray, and walked out as fast as she could.

....

"Why do we even have to teach Music Appreciation to a bunch of kids that aren't musicians," Tabitha grumbled to Michael over dinner.

"Isn't that precisely the group Music Appreciation is meant to reach?"

"Well yeah, but we don't have math appreciation or science appreciation. You just take algebra or biology. They should have to take piano or something. The only people that want to learn about composers and all that stuff *are* musicians—and not even all of them."

"Point taken. What about Richard Scott? Isn't Music History the only other class he teaches besides his private lessons? Get Nita to ask him."

"She did. He said—and I quote—'No, but hell no.' Told her he'd quit before he'd teach Music Appreciation."

"Well, maybe you should quit."

Tabitha's brows shot up. "I can't do that."

"I don't mean *really* quit. Just threaten to, like Scott." Tabitha opened her mouth but Michael held up his hand. "I know you won't. You're too responsible."

"Why does everyone make being responsible a bad thing? It wouldn't be right. And flute teachers are much easier positions to fill than good double-reed teachers. I know she needs me to, so... meet the new Music Appreciation instructor."

"Okay then. You'll do a great job." He took a bite of tofu.

"You don't know how much I dread it. Kids always hate that class."

"Then make it fun," Michael said, his mouth full. "What are we eating?"

"Leftover tofu covered in melted cheese." Tabitha scrunched up her face. "No one can make Music Appreciation fun, and you know it."

"Look, Tabby, if you said you'd do it, do it. If you don't want to, don't. But I don't want to listen to you whine about it the rest of the year."

Tabitha's brow furrowed. "You make me sound like I complain all the time."

He took her hand. "It's not that so much, although you do. But it would be nice if you stood up for yourself every once in a while. It's okay to say no."

Tabitha pushed her leftover tofu around her plate. He reached across the table and lifted her chin.

"Hey, do you want to order a pizza?"

"You don't like my healthy dinner?"

"I didn't like it yesterday and it's not better today. So, do you want pizza?"

"Can we get black olives?"

"For you, anything. As annoying as the whining is, you look adorable when you pout."

"I don't pout."

"Do you want the pizza?"

She batted her lashes at him. "Call that baby in."

Michael looked through his contacts for the pizza place.

"I think fixing you tofu gave me bad karma."

He looked up. "What?"

"Never mind. Just call. I'm starving. I didn't eat much lunch."

He covered the phone. "Pick-up or delivery? Delivery would give us time to—" he waggled his eyebrows.

"I'll pick it up." She could tell he was miffed and felt bad. "Hey, I'm just tired and hungry. Maybe afterward we could go to bed early?" She batted her lashes again, but he ignored her.

"After I eat I'm meeting the guys at the gym."

"Oh."

"It would have burned some calories."

"What would have?"

"Fooling around."

"Is that why you wanted to? You wanted to burn calories?"

'I was thinking of you. I know there's no way you would voluntarily exercise."

"You are telling me you wanted to mess around for my health." She looked for her keys. "I'm leaving to pick up the pizza. And I'm telling them to add extra cheese. And a two-liter of pop. Maybe a lava cake. No, two cakes. I'm going to get two."

"I don't want one."

She grabbed her purse. "Who said anything about sharing? Now I'll just waddle out, and if I can still fit inside the car I'll pick up the food."

Chapter 6
Dinner At Gran's

Atticus handed the laundry basket over, tipped his cowboy hat toward Tabitha, and climbed into his Ranger.

"Dinner's in five minutes," Gran called over her shoulder, the screen door banging shut behind her.

"Here, I'll take it." Tabitha reached for the laundry basket.

"I have it," the dark-haired man said. "I will take it up."

"No, please, it's embarrassing."

The man held it out. Tabitha took the basket and disappeared up the stairs.

"Dinner's ready," Mrs. Lovejoy called from the foot of the stairs. Tabitha didn't realize how hungry she was until she breathed in the aroma of enchiladas with green chiles.

"I hope you like Mexican food. My mother grew up in Juarez and it's what I learned to cook," said Mrs. Lovejoy as she filled the glasses with tea. The man sat, relaxed and waiting, his black braid hanging over the chair back. Tabitha sat in the empty chair, somehow managing to look both awkward and prim as Mrs. Lovejoy bustled about.

The man said, "Have a seat, Gran, you are making me dizzy. It smells great."

Gran? He looks too old to be her grandson.

"Tabitha, this is my boy, Nick. Nick, this is the new music teacher, Tabitha Peterson. She just got in. I guess you've already met," she said, chuckling.

"Hello," he said.

"Hi." Tabitha thought she saw a hint of something in his eyes. *Does this amuse you?*

"She took the spare apartment upstairs," Grand said, scooping enchiladas onto plates.

The corner of Nick's mouth twitched and Gran looked away, amused. The three ate in silence for a few minutes, before he asked, "Why was Atticus here?" Although he looked at his grandmother, Tabitha felt the question was directed at herself.

"Oh, there was an incident at the laundry mat. Let's not talk about it right now. Nick, would you pass the rice?"

Nick passed the rice but wanted answers. "Miss Peterson, what did Atticus want with you?"

Tabitha froze. "He, ah... I... um... there was a man in the dryer," she said, wild-eyed. Nick looked from her to his grandmother and back, bewildered. Tabitha folded her napkin. "I hate to be rude, but I'm afraid I need to be excused. Thank you for dinner." She hurried up the stairs.

Gran cuffed Nick on the back of his head. "I said not to talk about it."

"What is going on?"

"Vinnie is dead and Tabitha found his body."

Nick put his fork down and leaned back in his chair. "Whoa."

"Yeah. Not great dinner conversation." She shrugged. "Would you like a sopapilla? They're fresh."

Nick gave her a thumbs-up, never one to turn down a fresh-baked sopapilla.

·····•·····

The next morning Tabitha woke to the sound of the bathroom shower. *I guess my floormate is home. I hope she isn't a bathroom hog.* She waited until she heard the blow dryer shut off, then waited a few minutes more to ensure the bathroom was empty before she went in. After a shower, she went downstairs to find a full breakfast spread set out on the buffet. She'd smoothed her hair into a ponytail and put on a little blush to make a good impression on whoever she was sharing the bathroom with, and that, combined with a good night's sleep, made her look much cheerier than the previous night.

"Good morning," she said. "I thought the other renter might be down. Did she leave?" Nick, already working his way through a pile of eggs and bacon, could only nod, his mouth full of egg. She poured herself some coffee and inhaled the nutty aroma.

Mrs. Lovejoy bustled in with a bowl of fresh fruit.

"This is amazing. Thank you," said Tabitha, helping herself.

Mrs. Lovejoy filled her own plate before speaking. "I think we better go to the sheriff's office right after breakfast before Atticus shows up and hauls you off. You look nice. It stormed all night; did you sleep well?

"Yes. Much better than I have in a long time."

Mrs. Lovejoy chattered away the rest of the meal, although Nick ate without joining in.

Mrs. Lovejoy dabbed at her mouth with her napkin. "Let me get these dishes cleaned up and then we'll go."

Tabitha scooted her chair back and picked up her plate. "Let me help."

Nick reached across the table, taking the plate from Tabitha's hand. "I will do this. You two have someplace to be." Tabitha looked at him blankly, taken aback. Michael had certainly never offered to help with kitchen chores. *Well, technically he's offered, but I've never seen him actually do any.*

"Thank you, Nick. You're a good boy." Mrs. Lovejoy rose on her tiptoes as Nick bent down to accept her kiss on his cheek. "We should be back before lunch."

Once in the car, Tabitha asked, "Surely you don't make a big lunch, too?" Mrs. Lovejoy laughed. "No. Everyone is on their own for lunch." The temperature hovered around thirty-four, but Nick had started the car a few minutes before, and the old Buick felt warm and cozy as they drove. Tabitha relaxed, relieved that she and Mrs. Lovejoy were comfortable together without speaking. *I could like this place.* The car slowed and Tabitha opened her eyes to find they were pulling up to the sheriff's office. *Good night, I must have dozed off.*

"I'm going to drop you off while I run some errands. I'll wait for you in the cafe next door."

"I can walk back," Tabitha protested.

"That won't do. If Atticus makes you cry I won't have the new teacher walking home in tears again. Don't worry, there's always someone in the cafe to keep me company." She winked. "It's how I get all the good gossip."

Gravel crunched under the sedan tires as she backed out. Tabitha paused, one hand on the glass door. She took a deep breath, then pushed it open. A little bell tied to the handle tinkled. *They sure like bells around here.* No lights were on and she squinted, waiting for her eyes to adjust, wondering why Yaeleen was not at her desk. For the merest second, she wondered if maybe she'd come too early or they were eating breakfast at the cafe when a slight movement caught her eye. Atticus Blackhorn once again filled the doorway, the corridor behind him even darker. And from what she could see, he did not look happy.

Chapter 7

Office Visit

"Why aren't the lights on?" Tabitha blurted out.

"Yaleen doesn't get here until nine."

And you can't turn the lights on yourself?

"Come on back." He jutted his chin toward the hall before sauntering into the blackness. Tabitha hesitated.

"Are you afraid?" He asked, his voice low and, to Tabitha's ears, mocking.

"Of course not." *Hell yes, I'm afraid.* Nevertheless, Tabitha followed his voice down the darkened hall. The passageway took a sharp left, and light emanated from what must be his office. He sat behind an old oak desk. Two brown metal folding chairs were placed in front of the desk, their beige vinyl seats well-used. Tabitha chose the one nearest the door.

"I'd offer you coffee but, as I said, Yaeleen's not here yet."

"That's fine. I've already had some." She smiled, hoping he couldn't tell how nervous she felt.

"You nervous?"

Damn. "No. Why would I be?"

"Why would you, indeed?"

She looked around, determined to make him start the interview first. An old calendar on the wall displayed shiny new tractors, *Deeter's Tractor Supply* printed in large black letters across the top. That was it. No photos of family. Nothing that might give her anything at all to look at. Nothing to give her a hint about this man. She tapped her lip with her index finger. "I'm here. So, how does this work?" She could see it made him happy that she broke first.

"Just tell me what happened."

"You already know everything. I went to the laundromat to wash clothes and found him in the dryer. That's it."

"Okay," he said, leaning back in his chair. "Tell me a little about yourself."

"Um, I'm a music teacher. I moved here last week. What do you want to know?"

"Married or single?"

Is he smirking? "Divorced. I told you that yesterday. I have no idea why that might be pertinent."

"Yesterday you said 'divorced', but you also said 'married'."

Tabitha could feel her cheeks getting hot. "I am divorced."

"Well, *Mrs. Muckelroy*, I called the county and it appears you are very much married to a Mr. Michael Muckelroy. You introduced yourself as Tabitha Peterson."

"Ms. Peterson. I never took my husband's name, but I signed the divorce papers last week before I moved. Perhaps they haven't updated their records, but I assure you—I am divorced."

A telephone jangled in the front office, startling them both, then stopped mid-ring. Yaeleen must have come in.

"Okay. So let's go with 'divorced' for the time being. So you got divorced, got a new job, found a place to live, and moved to a new town, all in the space of a week. That's quick."

"I don't see how any of this has to do with the man in the dryer, or is any of your business at all."

Well, Mrs. Muckelroy—"

"*Ms.* Peterson."

"Well, *Ms.* Peterson, our music teacher went missing two weeks ago."

Her head snapped up. "They can't be related, can they?"

Ignoring the question, Atticus brushed imaginary lint from his uniform shirt before looking up, his eyes direct and intense, "And a man turns up dead the day you get here. Seems unusual, is all." He pressed on. "Have any family around here? I looked up your maiden name, but nothing turned up."

"No one. I didn't know about the music teacher, either. Are we finished?"

"For now. I know where to find you. Just don't leave town." The words were so cliché she looked up, expecting him to be joking, but it was clear he was anything but, judging by his demeanor.

Tabitha reached down to get her purse only to find the strap caught under a chair leg. She tugged hard and the purse sailed over the folding chair. She lunged for it as it hit the floor, then stood up too fast. The room began to spin and she grabbed for the chair, but in her haste to catch her purse, she'd knocked it over. Atticus barreled around the desk in a heartbeat. *He's lithe for such a big man,* then, *what an odd thought,* before her eyes fluttered and she crumpled against him, mortified.

"Yaeleen, I need you," he shouted over his shoulder.

Yaeleen lumbered down the hall to see Tabitha's face buried in Atticus's chest.

"Well."

"Please get Ms. Peterson a glass of water. And maybe a cold cloth for her head. But pull my chair around first."

Tabitha pushed away from him. "No, I'm fine. I don't need anything. I have to go." She swayed and put her hand out to steady herself.

He held her by her shoulders. "You're going to sit for a few minutes before you fall and bust your head open." Yaeleen rolled his old leather chair around, then went to the break room to look for a cloth. Atticus hooked his foot around the chair leg and pulled it close, then plopped Tabitha down into it. "Sit."

Tabitha decided that sitting for a few minutes might not be a terrible idea. Yaeleen came back with a wet cloth and handed it to Tabitha. She held it against her head for a few minutes, then handed it back. "I feel okay now." Tabitha stood again, willing herself not to wobble. "Thank you both." She fumbled around in her pocket for her new black gloves.

"I'll drive you home."

"No need. I'm meeting Mrs. Lovejoy at the cafe next door."

"Then I'm walking you over."

Her eyes flashed, and she hoped he hadn't noticed. *This man is a little too used to getting his way.* "I can manage."

"I'm not letting you go by yourself."

"You can't stop me."

Yaeleen, who had been studiously examining the floor during the exchange, made a small choking sound.

"You can either sit here or I'm going with you." Atticus grabbed his cowboy hat. "Yaeleen, I'll be at the cafe if you need me."

Oh brother.

Atticus took her arm, opened the door and steered her toward the cafe.

"You good?" He seemed genuinely concerned as they stopped at the entrance. She smiled up at him. His eyes were bright blue in the sun.

"Yes, thank you. This is extremely embarrassing."

"No worries." He headed back to the office.

"Hey, Sheriff?"

He stopped and turned to face her. "Atticus."

"Atticus, it just occurred to me. About the prior music teacher? You made it sound like there could be a link between the music teacher and Vinnie. I could be a spy or an informant or something. You know, your inside guy at the school."

It took three long strides to loom over her, his face tight. "Absolutely not. You don't know what you're talking about. You're a little girl. Hell, you just about fainted trying to stand up. You're a music teacher, Ms. Peterson. It's sweet. You're sweet. The kind of girl that wears pink lacies—I know, because I picked them up yesterday. But don't poke your nose where it doesn't belong. Yaeleen and I will handle this." It took a minute for him to relax, and then he smiled that lop-sided smile. "I have a crime to solve. Have a nice day."

·········

She opened the cafe door to the sound of the ever-present bell tinkling. Inside, it was bright and inviting. Framed photos of town events hung everywhere, with fresh daisies in little glass vases on every table. It was packed, and more than a few customers looked at her with curiosity. Tabitha could see that she would be plastering on her teacher face a lot in this town. Mrs. Lovejoy, sitting in a booth toward the back, saw Tabitha first and waved her over. True to her word, two women sat across from her. Mrs. Lovejoy picked up her purse and scooted over, patting the space beside her.

"Sit. I ordered you a piece of chocolate pie. It's homemade and delicious. Kelly owns the place and makes it from scratch." Mrs. Lovejoy caught the waitress's eye and held her coffee cup up. The teenager hustled over with a fresh pot of coffee. "River, this is the new music teacher, Ms. Peterson. Tabitha, this is River."

"Hi. It's good to meet you." Tabitha had never been introduced to a server before.

"Welcome to Medicine Creek. I'm glad you're here." The waitress couldn't have been more than fifteen, her thick black braid reaching to her waist, and Tabitha wondered if she was Native American. She turned Tabitha's cup right-side-up without asking and filled her cup, then topped off everyone else's.

"River plays flute. She's very good," said Mrs. Lovejoy.

"Oh, Gran," River said, looking at the floor.

"Well, it's true, and I expect that Ms. Peterson will agree as soon as she hears you play."

"I'm looking forward to it. I play flute also."

River kept her eyes averted but bobbed her head once, a small smile playing across her face. "Well, I better get moving. It's busy today," she said as another customer raised his cup.

"Is she your granddaughter?" Tabitha emptied a packet of sugar into her coffee.

"No, why—oh, because she called me Gran? Everyone calls me that. You should, too. No one calls me Mrs. Lovejoy. My husband and I were never blessed with children, but somehow I managed to become a grandmother to the entire town."

The woman across the booth spoke up. "Don't let her fool you. She wouldn't have it any other way. I'm Lenore, and this fine lady next to me is Estelle. I'll introduce us since Gran didn't bother to."

"Oh, hush, Lenore. I just hadn't gotten around to it. Tabitha, these are my sisters, Lenore and Estelle. Lenore is the old one," she said, her brown eyes sparkling. "There. Happy now?" Gran said primly.

Lenore laughed. "Yes. Oldest and wisest. You don't bother me, baby sister. Tabitha, we love this one to pieces, but she's a nut."

Kelly came over as the women were about halfway through their pie. "Hi. I just wanted to greet the new music teacher. I'm Kelly."

"Hi, I'm Tabitha. It's nice to meet you. And I have to say, this is the best pie I've ever had. It's delicious."

"I told her your pie is amazing." Gran picked up her purse. "It's good seeing you both, but I've got to get home and put my groceries away. Kelly, it's my turn to treat. Would you put it on my tab, please?" The sisters hugged one another and Tabitha followed Gran to the car, the bell tinkling behind them.

Once in the car, Tabitha had a question. "Mrs. Lovejoy?"

"Gran."

"Gran. You don't look old enough for Nick to be your son, but you introduced him to me as your boy. Is he related to you?"

Gran watched her rearview mirror as she backed out. "Nick's parents died young so he came to live with me."

"Poor Nick. That's so sad. But it's wonderful that you took him in."

Gran headed north. "I'm taking you around the town square to show you where things are. Most of the shops for the locals are on the northeast side, and the tourist spots are on the west, along the river. The school's up north, but I imagine you already know where it is."

Tabitha laughed. "It's the *only* place I know. I spent the entire week getting ready for school to start Tuesday."

"So you're ready?"

"As ready as I can be. I'll tell you a secret; I've never taught public school."

"You'll be fine. The kids here are a little rough around the edges, but they're good-hearted. You just need to polish them up." Gran pointed to her left. "There's the library, and right across the street is our little theatre. There's a lot of talent in our little town." Tabitha could hear the pride in her voice. Gran pointed to her right. "See that road? It leads east to the Blackhorn ranch. The Blackhorns pretty much run this town."

Tabitha heard something in Gran's voice that told her Gran might not be too happy about that. "Atticus Blackhorn?"

"His father. They own most of the land around here. They run cattle, but Atticus's grandfather found oil, and that's where their real wealth comes from."

Tabitha pondered this for a few minutes, then asked, "May I ask you something?"

"Sure."

" I know it's none of my business, but I'm curious. How did Nick's parents die?"

Gran's mouth set. "You're right. It is none of your business."

Tabitha's cheeks flamed. *How could I have asked such a personal question?*

"I am so sorry. I should never have asked. Please accept my apology."

Gran's voice softened. "I get protective when it comes to Nick."

Tabitha made a wry face. "Sometimes my curiosity gets the better of me."

Gran stared at the road. "And sometimes, Tabby, curiosity kills the cat."

Tabitha glanced over at the joke, her smile fading almost before it formed. Gran had a strange look on her face Tabitha couldn't decipher, but one thing was clear; she was not joking.

Chapter 8
Millie

They drove the rest of the way home in silence. Gran pulled into the gravel driveway and patted Tabitha's arm. "I can tell you've never lived in a small town before. We all get along, but we have the same problems as a big city, and we deal with things a little differently here. In a city, you can insulate yourself. You don't know every little thing that people do, every little problem they have. There's some anonymity in a city. We don't have that luxury here. Living in a small town is like living under a microscope. Take Vinnie. In a city, you read about a murder in the news, then you go about your day. But here—everybody in town knew Vinnie. I've known him since kindergarten. Things get real personal in a small town. So there are things we just don't talk about. You'll get used to us, but you've got to give us time to get used to you, too."

Gran shut the engine off, rifled through her purse, and pulled out a key. "And here's your key to the outside door.

You're always welcome to use the main door, but you might like a little anonymity sometimes." She smiled as she pressed the key into Tabitha's hand. "Tabby, I don't mean to scare you off. I am glad you're here."

'Tabby'. Somehow the nickname doesn't bother me when Gran says it. She hugged the older woman. "I appreciate it. You're right; I've never lived in a small town, and I think yours is charming."

"I love Medicine Creek, and you will too. Now remember, dinner is at six. Are you going to the school this afternoon? It starts Tuesday, right?"

"It does. I think I'll spend the rest of the day in my classroom, then relax tomorrow and look around the shops along the river. Get to know Medicine Creek a little better."

"Tomorrow is Sunday."

Tabitha looked at her, not understanding.

"Honey, Sunday is church day. All the shops will be closed."

"Oh. Then I'll look around today; I kind of need a break, anyway. The past two days have unnerved me a little, to be honest."

"There's a path by the river that's real pretty, but I wouldn't stay too long. Once the sun goes down it gets nippy that close to the water."

Tabitha found the path with no trouble. Medicine Creek nestled at the foot of the Wichita mountains, and she followed the path beside the river up to the shops. A few solitary joggers passed by, but other than that, Tabitha had the trail to herself. It hadn't gotten above forty-five degrees all day, but the walk warmed her. She pulled her hat off and stuffed it in her pocket, along with her black kid gloves, a Christmas present from Miki. Any gift from Miki was ridiculously expensive, and Tabitha would never spend that kind of money on herself, but she loved them and didn't want to risk getting them dirty.

The incline wasn't steep, but it was steady, and after a while, Tabitha unwound her scarf and unbuttoned her coat. She took deep breaths of the crisp winter air as she walked, willing her shoulders and neck to relax. The river burbled beside her, clear and sparkling, and though the trees were bare, Tabitha found it peaceful and beautiful. *I bet it's fabulous in summer.* Up ahead she could see the shops and decided to have a hot chocolate.

Halfway down the row of shops, a little cafe decorated in pinks and reds caught her eye, its holiday lights twinkling and inviting. A welcome wave of warmth and the smell of fresh-baked cookies rushed out as she opened the door. A young woman with shoulder-length red hair sat by the front window, her back to the counter. A teenage girl in a frilly pink apron came out of the back.

"Do you want something?" Somehow the frilly apron seemed incongruent with the girl's manner. Her eyes were ringed in black and Tabitha guessed she'd tried to dye her hair herself—presumably a bright red or orange—but now it resembled the color of a rusty old car.

'Do you have hot chocolate?"

The girl pointed to the chalkboard menu above her head. "Can you read?"

The woman by the window gave the girl a warning look. "Skye."

The girl sighed dramatically. "Yes," she said, a plastic smile plastered on her face. "Would you like some delicious hot chocolate? It's our specialty. The best in—"

"*Skye.*"

Skye rolled her eyes and went back into the kitchen.

"She's is working on her people skills," the woman said, her voice warm.

"Is she your employee?"

"Oh, no. She's one of my students." She smiled, her teeth even and white, a sprinkle of freckles dusting her nose and cheeks.

"So you're a teacher?"

"Yes. High school English."

"I'm Tabitha Peterson, the new music teacher."

"Great! I didn't know if they'd be able to find someone mid-year. I'm Millie. English, art, drama, and 'other duties as required'.

Tabitha laughed. "I know where you're coming from."

Millie patted the table. "Come sit if you're not busy, and tell me all about yourself."

"Thank you. Should I wait at the counter...?"

"She'll bring it to you."

Tabitha lowered her voice. "Should I drink it?"

Millie laughed. "It will be fine. Skye hasn't poisoned anyone in a week or two."

"At least not that you know of," Skye said, setting the hot chocolate down with a plate of butter cookies.

"These look delicious but I didn't order cookies."

Skye rolled her eyes up to the ceiling. "I *know*." Tabitha could hear her sigh again as she slunk away.

"That's her way of saying she's sorry," Millie laughed.

"I just ate a giant piece of chocolate pie at Kelly's Cafe. Will she be offended if I don't eat the cookies?"

Millie leaned forward, whispering conspiratorially, "Unless you know she's not in any of your classes, I would eat every bite."

"I think I'm up for the task, but you have to help. One of my goals in moving here is to get fit, but I can see now I may never lose weight in this town." She took a bite and closed her eyes. "Okay, these are amazing." She held out the plate. "Cookie?"

"Don't mind if I do. So what brought you to our humble town?"

"I saw the opening and I applied."

"Well, that's succinct."

"I didn't mean to be rude."

"No, no. Not at all. Now it's your turn to ask a question."

"I am curious why the former music teacher left."

"She was a first-year teacher, and I don't think she knew what she was in for. Have you ever taught in a rural community?"

Tabitha shook her head.

"It's different. Most of these kids have lived here their entire lives and are suspicious of outsiders. I think they gave her a hard time."

Tabitha leaned back, her eyes widening. "Are they that awful?"

"No, but I won't lie; they're a challenge. Stand your ground and you'll be fine."

"So she just packed up and left? Did she give notice?"

Millie leaned forward, her voice low. "No, she just vanished. The evening of the Christmas concert, she didn't show up, and no one's seen or heard from her since."

"How bizarre."

Millie made a face, then took a bite of cookie, nodding sagely. "The kids were still in the band room waiting to warm up while the entire town sat in the auditorium looking at a stage filled with empty chairs. It felt surreal. Actually, more than surreal—downright creepy." She flapped her hands. "But let's talk about you. Did your husband get a job here?"

A shadow passed across Tabitha's face as she sipped her hot chocolate. "There's no husband."

"Oh, goodness. I've pried. I'm terribly sorry. I'm always curious why people move here."

"Don't worry. It's—gosh, I hate to say this—but it's complicated." Tabitha smiled to reassure her, liking this nosy woman. "Have you lived here your whole life?"

"Oh no. I'm from Dallas. One of the local boys went to the same college I attended and we fell in love."

"Where did you go?"

"Texas A&M. We're Aggies through and through. You?"

"I went to a conservatory. Don't tell anyone, but I got alternate certification to teach public school."

"Well, there's no shame in that, and lord knows, Oklahoma needs teachers. Going away to college was Brent's big adventure, but he's a hometown kind of guy, so I made the move." Millie made a face, but hurriedly added, "I love it here. It's home."

Tabitha looked out the window. "I'm sure I will, too. It's charming. "

Skye began stacking chairs, then brought out a broom and began sweeping under their table.

"I think that's our cue," said Millie, laughing. "She wants to close up early. I'm sure she has big plans with her friends, not that she has many. Anyway, it's time to get home and make dinner. I can hear Brent's stomach growling as we speak."

"I better head back, too. It's getting late and I don't want to try to find my way back in the dark."

"Are you walking? Let me give you a ride."

"That'd be great if it's not out of your way."

"There is no such thing as 'out of the way' in Medicine Creek. Skye?"

"What?"

"Put it on my tab, will you, and I'll give you your tip Tuesday at school. I don't have any cash."

Tabitha pulled open her purse and handed Skye her credit card. "This is on me."

Skye looked at Millie, confused. Millie crinkled her eyes shut, trying not to laugh.

"Put it away. I've got it." When Tabitha protested, Millie laid her hand on her arm. "Tabitha, most shops here only take cash or checks."

"Checks? Who writes checks nowadays?" asked Tabitha.

Millie giggled and patted Tabitha on the back. "Welcome to Medicine Creek, new friend!" Once outside, Millie pointed to a cute yellow Beetle parked about five shops down. "I parked in front of the dress shop. I wanted something sparkly to wear tonight."

"It sounds like you have a special night planned. What's the occasion?"

"It's New Year's Eve, honey. Don't tell me you forgot?"

"I guess I did. I spent Christmas with my mother, got here Monday, and it's been a crazy week."

"I can see that. What with you and Agnes finding Vinnie's body, you're the talk of the t—" Millie's hand flew to her mouth when she caught Tabitha's horrified expression. "Oh my gosh, I am so sorry. I can't believe I said that."

"It's fine. There's a lot to talk about." An icy wind gusted at the top of the hill now that the sun had set. Tabitha buttoned her coat and reached into her pocket, pulling out a single glove. She stuck her hand in her other pocket. Nothing. "Oh dear, I must have left my glove and scarf inside. My mother knitted it for me. Do you mind waiting?"

"Not at all."

Tabitha tried the door but it was locked. She peered inside to see Skye sweeping up and tapped on the glass. Skye opened the door.

"What?"

"I dropped my scarf and a black glove; did you happen to find them?"

"No." Skye closed the door. Tabitha hurried back to the Beetle.

"You couldn't find it?"

Tabitha shrugged. "Oh well. I'm a little old for pink and white poms anyway."

Millie backed out. "So you don't have any plans? I'm having a big party and you have to come. It'll be a great way for you to meet everyone and put those rumors to rest."

"There are rumors?"

"Good night, I've done it again. Don't you worry about it. It's a small town and people have nothing better to do. Just think of it as a chance to wear something shiny."

Tabitha shook her head. "I don't think so. It's kind of you to ask, but I'm going to pass this time."

"You have to come. As your new best friend, I insist." Millie grinned, waggling her finger.

"Under the circumstances, a quiet evening with a good book and a hot cup of tea is what I'm looking forward to."

Millie touched Tabitha's arm. "In all seriousness, you need to come. All the important people in town are expected to be there, and they're eager to meet you. If you don't come it will only fuel more gossip."

"I don't have anything suitable to wear."

"Come early. Wear a pair of black pants and I'll loan you a blouse. I think we're about the same size." She raised her eyebrows and put on her best teacher voice. "I'm not taking 'no' for an answer, young lady."

"I'll put in an appearance, but I won't stay long."

"Wonderful! I'm an amazing cook. You'll have fun, I promise." Tabitha doubted that, but she did know that, as a teacher in a small town, there were certain expectations.

"And tomorrow we're all getting together for a New Year's Day run."

"Oh no. I have a firm do-not-exercise policy. I've never been the slightest bit athletic and have no plans to start now. A run is a hard no."

"Okay. But you are coming to my party."

······

As they pulled into the driveway, they could see Nick, his foot resting on a porch rail.

"Ooh, that man is something. Have you talked to him yet?"

"Yes. He seems nice, but he's not much of a conversationalist." Tabitha wasn't sure where the conversation was going but tried to steer clear of where she thought it might end up. She opened the car door before Millie could say anything more. "Thank you for the ride. I'll see you tonight." Halfway to the porch, she loped back to the car before Millie could put the Beetle in reverse.

"I'll ride with Nick; I assume he knows where you live?"

"Ooh, you're going to ask Nick for a ride?" Millie smiled broadly.

"I assume he's attending."

Millie's smile faded. "Um, Nick won't be there."

"I thought you said the whole town is coming."

Millie took a deep breath. "He's not invited."

"Why?" Tabitha blurted out without thinking.

"Because—Atticus. I'm late. See you there." She backed out before Tabitha could ask any more questions and gunned the Beetle, gravel flying as she sped away.

Because—Atticus? What did that mean?

Chapter 9
The Party

"Good evening, Nick," Tabitha said as Millie drove away. Nick tilted his head in Tabitha's direction. *Saving your energy, huh?* Now that the sun had set, the porch filled with shadows, making it difficult to discern his features. The screen door squeaked open and Gran stuck her head out.

"Dinner will be ready in ten minutes." The old wooden door bounced against its frame as Gran bustled back in. Tabitha mounted the steps and crossed the porch, but stopped short of the door.

"Nick? I know I'm being nosy, but is there bad blood between you and Atticus?" She wished she could see his face. She could hear Gran humming in the dining room. Tabitha felt his eyes burning into her, then dismissed the thought as ridiculous. The silence was unsettling, and after another beat, she went upstairs to wash up.

The smell of fresh bread drifted up the stairs as she made her way down. *How can I still be hungry? All I've done today is eat.*

"Sit down before it gets cold," said Gran. "Oh, my stars, I forgot the potatoes. Please, go ahead and serve yourselves."

Nick helped himself to two pork chops as Tabitha spooned peas onto her plate, the silence palpable. She reached across the table for the basket of bread just as he reached for the bowl of peas and their hands brushed against each other. She snatched her hand back as fast as she could and knocked over Gran's crystal candlestick. It toppled off the table, but Nick caught it before it hit the floor.

"You're quick, Nick," Gran quipped as she set the mashed potatoes on the table.

"I'm so sorry. I can be extremely clumsy at times," said Tabitha.

"Don't worry. Nick always saves the day. Don't you, Nick?" Gran said, her voice full of affection.

His expression softened when he looked at her. "I do what I can, Gran."

"Tabitha, did I see Millie's little Beetle pulling away? I believe she married that Sawyer boy. She's new and fits right in. A real nice young woman."

"Gran, she has lived here for five years," said Nick.

"That's new around here." Gran laughed. "Nick, do you have any plans for tonight?"

"I am going celebrate the new year with you."

"Tabitha?"

"Millie's invited me to her home."

"Oh, that big fancy party she has every New Year's Eve. That should be fun."

"I'm not sure I'm going. I'm tired, and I lost a glove. After dinner, I'm going down to the river and see if I can find it, then call it a night."

"No you will not!" Gran slapped the table playfully. "You're going to that party, young lady. I'll drive you myself."

"But Gran, the gloves are new and a gift from a friend. I really want to find it."

"What does it look like?"

"It's black kid leather."

"Nick will look for it, won't you, Nick?" Nick did not look thrilled. "Go upstairs and get yourself ready while I put the leftovers away, then I'll drive you over."

·····•·····

Millie's house sat east of town, on the same street as the Blackhorn place. The manicured lawn stretched from the road well past the house to what looked to be stables. The house itself, larger and more elegant than Tabitha would have guessed, exuded country charm. Millie answered the door dressed in red sequins and diamonds. Tabitha felt frumpy beside her in the black slacks and cream silk blouse she'd chosen. She'd pulled her hair back in a low ponytail and tied it with a velvet ribbon, and even put on the red Chanel lipstick she saved for special occasions. It was the most festive outfit she had and she felt pretty—until Millie opened the door.

"Come in, come in! I'm so glad you're here. People are trickling in and they're going to want to talk your ear off. Let's get you upstairs and into something sparkly."

"Millie, I appreciate it, but I'm fine wearing this."

"Nonsense, you look like you're on your way to work. Come on, we're gonna gussy you up!"

Tabitha looked askance, and Millie instantly backed off. "Oh my, I've offended you. You look wonderful how you are. Understated elegance."

"I'm not used to glam, Millie. You can pull this sort of thing off," Tabitha said generously.

"Tabitha, I look like a tart and I know it, but my dear husband is under the impression this is how high-class women dress. Wait until you see his mother. You'd think she raided Dollie Parton's closet. In the dark. This get-up is tame compared to hers." Millie's laugh was infectious and Tabitha relaxed.

Millie pointed toward a group of teachers standing by a huge rock fireplace. "There's your tribe. Let me get you something to drink and introduce you. Most of them are nice.

Honestly, I'd rather hang out with them, but I am the hostess, so I need to circulate. After all, I am a social butterfly." Millie giggled and batted her fake lashes coquettishly. She returned with two glasses and handed Tabitha one, then stuck her hand up, waving to get one of the teacher's attention. She maneuvered through the crowd, smiling and waving like everyone was her best friend as Tabitha trailed along in her wake.

"This is Sue. She teaches all the sciences, and this is Ethan, the baseball and basketball coach. He also teaches history." Millie looked around. "Where's Coach Randall?"

"He couldn't make it. Said something about a stomach bug," said Ethan.

"Oh. Too bad. Anyway, he's the football coach. And last but not least, this is Barbara. She teaches algebra and geometry, and is the sanest of the bunch." Millie winked at a big woman with long brown hair streaked with gray.

"We're going to play cards," Barbara said, then lowered her voice. "It's a great way to look like you're getting to know everyone without having to actually converse."

"I'm all in," said Tabitha, instantly liking her. The woman looked competent and easy in her skin, and Tabitha wondered if she'd lived here all her life. *She looks strong, like she rides horses or lives on a ranch. I'm going to like it here. These people are down-to-earth. They know who they are and where they came from. Miki and Zamarri would be appalled.*

Tabitha settled down to a rowdy game of cards with her new friends, then excused herself early, having already made arrangements with Gran to pick her up at ten o'clock. After saying her goodbyes, Tabitha made her way outside, where the old sedan sat idling.

"Thank you so much for rescuing me," she said as she opened the car door and fell into the seat, fumbling for her seat belt in the dark. "They were playing music so loud I think my ears started to bleed. And I had no idea there were so many sequins in Medicine Creek." She clicked the seat belt triumphantly. "There!" She leaned her head back against the seat and closed her eyes, still talking. "I saw Atticus but he didn't speak to me. Don't tell anyone, but I think he's a little full of himself; maybe it's all that oil money you were telling me about. And Gran, I know I'm just being nosy, but I am so curious. What's the deal between him and Nick?" She rolled her head towards the driver's side and opened her eyes to see Nick's face shrouded in shadow.

"You are right. You are nosy."

Tabitha was glad for the dark because she could feel how hot her cheeks were. "I am so sorry. Oh my god. I'm so sorry. I thought Gran was picking me up."

"Stop." As he put the car in gear and drove the length of the circle drive, Tabitha couldn't believe what a fool she'd made of herself. She covered her face with her hands, so didn't see him smiling. The drive back, painfully silent, felt like hours. When they pulled into the driveway Tabitha opened the door, ready to leap from the car.

"Tabitha, wait. Gran bought some champagne and made a snack to ring in the New Year."

"Mmm... I think I'll just go upstairs and read in bed. This week has been exhausting." *There is no way I can look you in the eye tonight.*

"It would mean a lot if you would make an appearance." Nick held out his hand and Tabitha felt her pulse increase. *Does he want to hold my hand?*

"Sure," said Tabitha. She felt like some shy, silly teenager as she put her hand in his. She felt something in it.

"Is this your glove? I found it down by the river."

"Oh. Yes. Right. Good." Tabitha dashed into the house and up the stairs. Nick sauntered onto the porch and leaned against the porch rail, smiling into the dark.

············

Tabitha flopped down on her bed. *I can't do this.* She pulled out her phone and stared at it, trying to decide who to call. Miki would no doubt be doing something glamorous. Tabitha felt too embarrassed to tell Nita, and she didn't want to even think of what Michael might be doing. *Mom, it is.*

"Happy New Year's Eve!" Only her mother would answer the phone like that.

"Happy New Year's Eve, Mom."

"How are you? I thought you would be at a party or something with all your new friends."

All my new friends. "I went to a party for a while, and my landlord has made a treat for us at midnight."

"So what's wrong?"

"Nothing's wrong, Mom. I'm just calling."

"Of course something's wrong. I can hear it in your voice."

Tabitha couldn't decide whether to laugh or cry, convinced her mother had some kind of mom ESP or something. *I can't tell her I found a body in the laundromat, or that the last music teacher went missing, or that the whole town is talking about me. Or that I'm terrified I might be attracted to a man who lives with his grandmother and has no job—and the sheriff thinks I might be a murderer.* She sat up and scooted back against the headboard. "Mom, I think I made a big mistake. I shouldn't have moved away." Tears formed and she squeezed her eyes shut.

"So why did you?"

"I wanted a fresh start. Somewhere calm, where no one knew me, so I could breathe. Figure things out." Tears flowed down her cheeks. "But it's not calm and I can't figure anything out. Michael was right. You were right. I should have moved in with you. Maybe Michael will take me back. I can call Nita in the morning and see if she's filled my position. I'm coming home."

"Oh no you are not, young lady. You are staying right where you are and finishing what you started. The only thing wrong with you is listening to me and Michael too much. You will stay, and you will be successful."

Tabitha sat up, shocked. "Mom, you *always* want me to come home. And all you talk about is how I should get back with Michael. How I need Michael."

"Well, not this time. I worry about you and always think someone should take care of my baby girl, but that's wrong. I am proud of you for leaving, and you are not coming back home."

"But what should I do? This is too hard."

"Go for a walk, take a shower, then go celebrate New Year's with your landlord."

Tabitha rolled her eyes. "I don't mean right this minute, Mom."

"Well, that's my advice. You can figure it out. I finally see that you don't need to be taken care of, but you have to see it, too. Oops, someone's at the door. Gotta go."

"At this hour? Don't answer it."

"Of course I'm going to answer it. It's my date. I love you and I have faith in you. Happy New Year!"

Your date? Tabitha tossed her phone on the bed and hung up her clothes. *My mother has a date for New Year's Eve. Can life get any weirder?* Tabitha looked out the window, restless. She heard the shower running. *My mystery roommate must be home. Well, Mom, I guess I'm going for a walk.* She threw on a pair of jeans and pulled a sweatshirt over her head, grabbed her coat, and peeked down the stairs, hoping to avoid Nick.

Once outside, she picked up her pace. *My mother thinks I can do this. I'm smart and resourceful. After all, I survived Michael. I found a new job and moved here with no help from anyone. Piece of cake. I've got this.*

Nick watched from his window, then grabbed his jacket and followed her.

Chapter 10
New Year's Eve

The moon lit the path. It was satisfying to hear the crunch of leaves under her feet. The temperature had dropped, but the wind had died down and Tabitha found the cold air invigorating. *My mother believes in me.* Tabitha fastened the top button of her coat, surprised to feel happier than she had in a long time. *My mother believes in me.* She thrust her hands in her pockets as she neared the river. The moon's reflection created silvery ripples on the water. *It's beautiful. Peaceful. I can make a life here.* She spotted a trail leading to the bank and picked her way down. Her footsteps made a squishy, quiet, sandpapery sound in the sandy loam. She looked up at the night sky, amazed to see so many stars with the moon so bright.

"It's awesome, isn't it?"

The voice jolted Tabitha from her reverie. She looked around to find Skye sitting on a large rock at the river's edge. Tabitha could feel her heart pounding as she turned her gaze first toward Skye, then to the moonlight reflecting in the river. "It is."

"You don't see this kind of sky in the city. It's the only thing I like about this place."

"You're not from here?"

Skye scrunched up her face. "*No,*" she said adamantly.

"What brought you here, if you don't mind me asking?"

Skye threw her a sharp look. "My mother."

"Do you have family in Medicine Creek? Or did she get a job here?"

"You are nosy."

"So I've been told." Tabitha decided not to ask any more questions of this strange girl.

"Listen," Skye whispered.

Tabitha tilted her head but heard nothing particular. "What am I listening for? Do you hear someone?" She looked around, a little nervous.

"*No.* Close your eyes and *listen,*" Skye said, the answer obvious–at least to her.

Tabitha closed her eyes. She heard the muffled sound of a lone car on Main Street. Not that. She took a breath and listened as a musician. There. The river. She lost herself in it for a few minutes before Skye interrupted.

"You hear it, don't you."

'The river."

"Yeah, it sings a song, and it's never the same."

Tabitha looked at her, curious. *What an odd girl.* "So that's why you come down here? To listen?"

"Yeah." Skye glanced down at the notebook in her lap.

"What's that?" Tabitha asked.

"You ask a lot of questions. I don't answer to you."

Tabitha frowned but decided to ignore it. "Do you draw?"

"No."

Tabitha waited to see if the girl would continue if she didn't press. It worked.

"I write words. Lyrics to the river songs."

"That's lovely."

Skye rolled her eyes.

"It is. You have an artist's heart."

"I just told you I don't draw."

"I mean an artist, as in someone who creates art. Any art. Music, dance... lyrics." She paused, then added, "I'm an artist. A musician."

"You're a music teacher. Not the same thing."

Ouch. That hits a little too close to home. "I am a music teacher, but first I am a musician."

Skye rolled her eyes again.

Hope they don't stick like that. "I teach to pay my bills," Tabitha blurted out. *Why did I say that? I don't owe her an explanation.*

"So you don't care about us. Figures." Skye jumped off the rock. "Gotta go."

"Skye, wait."

The girl stopped but kept her back to her.

"Look, everyone has to eat. There's no shame in that, and it doesn't mean I don't love what I do."

"Good to know. See you in class, Teach."

'See you in class?' Great. She's my student. What a start. Surely they can't all be as hard as Skye? Tabitha sat on the rock Skye had vacated, trying to get back the glow she'd felt after her mother's call. She closed her eyes and listened to the river, but couldn't force herself to recreate the mood. She leaned back on the rock, looked up at the sky, and blew out air. *A full moon on the first day of school.* Every teacher knew what that meant. *It's cold out here.* She felt in her pocket for her phone to check the temperature, then remembered she'd tossed it on her bed. *Oh well, it's too cold for me, whatever the temperature.*

The wind picked up. She jammed her hands in her pockets, walking fast and looking for her glove, trying to work up some body heat. *My neck is freezing. Wish I had my scarf. This cold is miserable.* The wind whistled through the bare trees and brush, and she didn't hear it until she paused to pull her collar up. *Something is in the bushes.* She strained to hear it again, but all she heard was the wind. *Must be a dog or something.* She picked up her pace, still listening, but the wind was howling now. *I wonder what kind of wild animals are around here. Just get back to the house. Don't think about it.* She stopped again despite herself, listening. There it was. It sounded like something walking, something upright. *Does Oklahoma have bears? Stop it—it's a dog.* She could see lights in the distance and breathed a sigh of relief. *It's a dog. It's just a dog. That's what it is. A big, stalker dog that walks like a full-grown man.*

She sprinted across the backyard, away from the woods and the giant-stalker-dog-man. *I just want a hot shower, a cup of tea, and hide under the covers.* She was almost to the front porch when she remembered the key to the outside door and ran up the outside stairs. The key turned easily in the lock and Tabitha opened the door to a brightly lit kitchenette, with Nick Spotted Wolf standing at the sink washing dishes in a pair of sweatpants. Only sweatpants.

"I see you got your key."

Tabitha tried to get her bearings. "What are you doing here?"

He held up the soapy rag and a plate. "Washing dishes."

"Huh." It was the best she could do.

His face didn't move, yet he managed to look amused.

"I assume Gran did not tell you that you have to go through my kitchen to get to your room."

"Nope," Tabitha said, popping the 'p'. *Did I just say 'nope'?*

Nick pointed to a door by the refrigerator. "That door opens to the landing at the top of the stairs."

Tabitha stood rooted to the floor.

He put the rag down and dried his hands, then leaned back against the counter, arms across his chest. "You're staring."

Oh my god, I am staring. Tabitha turned bright pink.

"Still staring."

"No I'm not."

He smiled. *He has a dimple.* Tabitha averted her eyes but didn't know where to look. She looked at the door she'd just come through. The tiny kitchen table covered with a pink floral tablecloth. The cupboard. His bed.

"Gran made that quilt for me for my tenth birthday."

Oh my god, he saw me looking at his bed.

"What are you thinking?" he asked.

"Why don't I have a kitchen?" *Where did that come from?*

He whirled his index finger in a circle. "Because this entire floor used to be mine until you came."

"So this was a two-bedroom apartment?"

"Nope." He popped the 'p' but didn't smile.

"So am I staying in your bedroom?" *I can't believe that just came out of my mouth.*

He didn't say a word but she thought the corner of his mouth might have twitched.

"I thought you lived with Gran." *I'm blathering.*

"I do live with Gran. This is her house."

"Of course. I don't know what I'm thinking." Her gaze flickered to his arms and bare chest.

Nick grinned. "Would you like me to guess?"

"*No*," she said louder than she meant, then blushed again. "I mean, I want to shower."

Nick's eyes widened.

"No. I.. I'm…" Tabitha felt hot tears threaten to spill over. Nick's smile disappeared. He crossed the kitchenette and held the door open for her.

"I will see you downstairs after your shower."

She looked up at him as she walked under his arm, sure he was mocking her, but his smile seemed genuine, and she nodded, grateful.

She grabbed a towel and turned the shower on as hot as she could stand. Steam filled the air. *This is where Nick showers.* She closed her eyes and let the water pummel her back, then washed her hair, her mind drifting. *This is too much.* She thought of her mother's words. *Mom, I think you may have a little too much faith in me.* She towel-dried her hair and looked in the mirror. Little curls were already springing up around her face. *Oh well, they can deal with it. I am not doing my hair at eleven-thirty at night.* She pulled her favorite sweater out and pulled it over her head. It was old and pilled, but she loved the pale blue color and the feel of cashmere on her skin. She dug through her toilette kit. *Just a hint of perfume, and maybe lipstick. And mascara, but that's all. It's not like I'm trying to impress anyone.*

She headed down to the little New Year's Eve party Gran was setting up. For just three of them, there was quite a spread, with cheeses, crackers, fresh fruit chunks, and homemade sugar cookies.

"Nick, would you get the champagne?" Gran hollered over her shoulder.

"May I help?" Tabitha asked as the doorbell rang.

"Would you mind getting the door?"

Tabitha sighed. *Who else did Gran invite? I thought it was just going to be the three of us.* She stretched her neck from side to side, plastered on her teacher face, and opened the door. Atticus Blackhorn filled the doorway, and he did not look in the mood to celebrate.

His eyes bored into Tabitha's. "Where were you tonight?"

Chapter 11
No. 2

Atticus's question took Tabitha aback. "Here and there. Why?"

"There's been another murder." Atticus took a step inside the door. Nick crossed the dining room to the entry hall in a second.

"Who was it?"

"We aren't releasing the name yet." Tabitha stepped back involuntarily, bumping against Nick's chest. Both men reached out to steady her, all the while glaring at one another. Tabitha, sandwiched between them, had never felt so tiny. And claustrophobic. Gran saw her distress and rushed over.

"You two oafs need to step back. You're crushing her." Gran pushed them toward the door. "If you're going to start bucking up, you can both take your little contest out in the yard. Come here, child, and sit down." Gran steered Tabitha to the nearest dining room chair and glanced toward the front door.

Without Tabitha between them, the men gave the distinct appearance of squaring off.

"You heard what I said. Both of you calm down or go outside. But close that door. You're letting all the heat out."

Nick had his hand on the door. "You heard her. I need to close the door."

"And I am on official business," Atticus said evenly.

"Let him in, Nick. The man's doing his job." Gran patted Tabitha's shoulder. "You okay?"

"I'm fine," Tabitha lied.

"Good. Then everyone come to the table and eat my dessert while we sort this out."

"Gran, this is business. I don't have time for—"

"My stars, Atticus, make time. You bang on my door at eleven-thirty at night, tell us someone's been killed, imply that our new music teacher has something to do with it, and then you say you don't have *time*? Sit. And take that cowboy hat off in my house."

Atticus set his hat on the table and sat across from Tabitha, with Nick to her right. Gran, who always sat at the head of the table nearest the kitchen, cut into her famous chocolate bundt cake.

"So, Atticus, tell us what's going on." Gran handed out slices of cake.

"We found another body." He rubbed his face. "Down by the river. And someone said they saw someone that looked like Ms. Peterson there." His eyes cut to Tabitha. "So—were you there?"

"Yes."

"What time?"

"Around four."

Nick's eyes flitted toward her, then took a bite of cake.

"Why were you down there?"

"I wanted to take a walk. Clear my head."

"Did you see anyone?"

"A jogger, but other than that, no one." For some reason, she didn't want to involve Skye. *And technically I'm not lying. I didn't see anyone on the way.*

"And then you came straight back here. What time?"

"I didn't come straight back. I went to that little cookie place."

"The Sweet Shoppe? Did anyone see you there? Anyone that could verify that you were there?"

"Yes. The waitress. And I shared a table with a woman named Millie."

"Millie Sawyer? And then you walked back? What time would that be?"

"Millie gave me a ride here about an hour later."

"And what did you do after that?"

"I got ready for Millie's party. You saw me there."

Atticus wrote something in a notebook.

"How did you get home?"

"I picked her up around ten p.m.," Nick interrupted, "And she's been with me ever since."

Tabitha's head jerked around. "No I have not."

Atticus cocked his head, waiting for her to continue, but Nick jumped in again.

"Well, okay. Not the entire time. She did take a long, hot shower."

"And how would you know that?"

Nick's eyes glinted. "We share a bathroom."

Atticus glared at him steely-eyed before turning his attention back to Tabitha. "So there was a period you were unaccounted for."

Tabitha's eyes grew large. "I guess so."

"That is not correct." Nick took Tabitha's hand. "I was in the bedroom, but I heard her singing the whole time. It was cute." She tried to take her hand back without drawing attention, but he held her with a vice-like grip.

Atticus turned his attention to Nick. "So where were you this evening?"

"Nick and I were playing cards all evening—except for when he picked up Tabitha," said Gran. "So I'm the only one without an alibi." Gran held out her plump little wrists. "Am I under arrest?"

Atticus's chair scraped against the wooden floor. "You three can play games as long as you want, but sooner or later I'm going find out what you're up to. Two bodies in the space of a week. There is a killer on the loose, and I'm going to catch whoever it is. Gran, thank you for the cake." He grabbed his hat and opened the front door. "And Ms. Peterson, don't go walking by yourself, even in the daytime."

"I don't have a car, and I have to get to work. I can take care of myself."

"No, you can't. You're five feet tall and all of one hundred pounds soaking wet. This is no joke. Bodies are piling up and we don't know who is responsible. Do you have a gun?"

"No!" said Tabitha, visibly shaken.

"I hate to ask, but—Nick?"

"I do. And I will not let her out of my sight."

"Make sure you don't." Atticus put his hat on. "Well, take care. And Gran, keep your doors locked for once."

....

Tabitha put a forkful of cake in her mouth, her head spinning. *Why did Nick and Gran lie? And why did Nick purposely give Atticus the impression something is going on between us?*

Gran took the dessert plates to the kitchen and returned with three delicately etched crystal champagne flutes.

Holding the flute to the light, Tabitha said, "These are gorgeous. Are they antique?"

"They were my great-grandmother's. The one luxurious thing she ever owned. I treasure them." She smiled at some unspoken memory, then said, "Nick, will you pour?"

Somehow I never pictured these two drinking champagne.

He poured champagne into each glass. "Toast?"

Gran lifted her glass, clinking it against Nick's. "To a prosperous and happy New Year." Tabitha's flute sat untouched. Nick watched as a myriad of emotions played over her face.

"Tabitha?" He tilted his flute toward her but, her face pensive, she left it alone.

Eyes on the table, she asked, "Why did you both lie?"

Neither answered. Nick set his champagne down. Tabitha lifted her face and looked from one to the other. Gran held Nick's eyes as he shook his head back and forth.

"What is going on?"

Nick set his glass down. "Happy New Year, Gran. Tabitha." The front door slammed as he left.

"It's getting late. Happy New Year, Tabitha. See you in the morning." Gran picked up the flutes.

"Mrs. Lovejoy—Gran—stop. I deserve to know. You both misled the sheriff in a murder investigation, and you caught me up in your lies. Are you two involved somehow?"

Gran sat down heavily. "No, Tabitha, of course we aren't. Things get complicated in a small town, and sometimes it's best to play your hand close to the vest. Wait and watch before you jump in." She patted Tabitha's hand reassuringly. "Don't worry about it. It will all work out."

"But Gran, if you have nothing to hide, why lie?"

"Because... because... well—Atticus. Sweetie, I'm feeling my age. I'll see you in the morning." She shuffled across the living room to her bedroom, and, for the first time, Tabitha thought Gran looked worn out.

··········

She lay in her bed, thinking of all the peculiar things happening since her move to Medicine Creek. *Is it too much to want a nice, quiet ordinary life? This town is a nut-house. No one seems to trust Atticus. Is he a loose cannon? His family runs the town; is that why he's sheriff? Is he unstable? A murderer is running loose.*

A door opened and closed. A minute later the toilet flushed. *I guess Nick's going to bed.* She shivered and pulled the quilt higher around her neck although she wasn't cold. *At least I'm safe with Nick in the room next to me.* She nestled back into her covers, willing her muscles to relax. As she drifted to sleep, a thought sprang into her head and her eyes popped open. *Atticus didn't tell us who the murder victim is. I wouldn't know them anyway.* Tabitha closed her eyes, drifting off again, then bolted upright. *Oh my god—did they lie because Nick is the killer?* She threw the covers off and tip-toed to lock her doors. *Am I sleeping in the room next to a murderer?*

Chapter 12

First Day of School

Atticus had not yet released the victim's name, and rumors were flying. Nick drove Tabitha to school as promised, an awkward silence hanging between them. *Surely he can't know I have doubts about him?* Nick pulled up at the student drop-off, and Tabitha felt ridiculous as she gathered her things.

"Shall I pick you up here at four?"

"No need. I can walk—" She caught sight of the set of his chin. "Or I can catch a ride."

"I will pick you up here at four."

It wasn't worth the fight. "Okay, thanks. But go to the back, please. This entrance is for students."

He nodded once and drove away. *I wonder what he does all day? He obviously doesn't have a job.* Thoughts of Nick vanished as she made her way to the front office to sign in. Office staff, students, and teachers bustled in and out, looking at her with varying degrees of curiosity, making Tabitha wonder if her peach blouse, black slacks, and black leather ballet flats were too casual. She took a few surreptitious glances around, her eyes stopping at a tall, thin, older woman wearing a lace-edged camouflage tee shirt with skin-tight jeans and red cowboy boots, her bright orange hair teased and piled high on her head. *I can safely rule out underdressed.* She heard a familiar trill and looked around to see Millie writing her name on the sign-in sheet, an entourage surrounding her.

"Tabitha!" Millie yelled over the din.

Tabitha waved and made her way over to her new-found friend. "I guess the first day back is always a little chaotic, no matter where you teach."

Millie looked confused, then laughed. "It's like this every day." Someone called her name, and she waved. "See you at lunch."

Tabitha found her way to the music room. *It's not a music room; it's a band room. I have to remember that. The principal seemed confused when I asked to see the music room.* The sounds of percussion exploded from within. *Who let the kids in unsupervised? That's a recipe for disaster.* She stopped at the doorway, mouth agape. Teenagers were everywhere. Some, already seated, were warming up, but most stood around, laughing and visiting. A boy and girl were making out in the far corner while across the room, three girls clustered around a cell phone, giggling and pointing. A group played drums against the back wall. It sounded to Tabitha like each drummer was playing a distinctly different cadence. *Is this the drumline the principal bragged about?*

"Hey," a tall boy holding a trombone yelled above the din, pointing toward Tabitha. "Hey," he shouted again, even louder. "The new band director is here."

Tabitha snapped her mouth shut and stuck on her most pleasant teacher face as she strode to the podium and faced sixty teens. *I'd rather be facing a pack of wolves. What was I thinking? I've never taught band. They must have been desperate to have hired me.*

"Hello. I'm Ms. Peterson, your new director. I'm glad to be here." Two clarinet players had their heads close together, whispering and cutting their eyes toward her. Tabitha ignored them and plunged on. "I'd like to dive right in, so please take your seats. I saw several warm-up and technique books in the cabinet. Which ones are you using?" Blank stares.

"What's that?" A saxophone player asked. A trumpet player laughed.

She turned to the trumpet player. "So, no books? What warm-up do you do?"

"We just—start."

"No long tones?"

"No."

"No scales?"

"No."

"No—"

"We just *start*." He stared at her, adamant.

"Ah. Good to know. I'll look around and have a warm-up for you tomorrow." Groans echoed around the band room. *Keep it moving, keep it moving.* "Let's begin with you playing something for me—maybe from your last performance?"

"We didn't get to have our last performance. The other band director bailed."

Tabitha took a deep breath. *Never let them see you sweat.* "Then play the concert. It will give me a chance to see where you're at, and where we need to go next." Once they began, Tabitha knew exactly where they were going—back to the beginning. The music was much too difficult. Her students at the Academy could handle this level, but not these kids.

The band room door banged open. "You guys suck. Bad. I think my ears are bleeding. I bet that's what happened to Miss Reed. She ran away before she died of embarrassment."

"Good morning, Skye."

"Is it, though?" Dressed in black from head to toe, she sauntered in, pushing open horn cases out of her way with a Doc Martin-clad foot. "No one got me a chair?" The flute players studied their music like they'd never seen it before, except for one. It took Tabitha a minute to place her—the waitress from the cafe, River. She sat first-chair, staring at Skye until Skye looked away.

Do I call her out or let it slide? Tabitha thought hard as she read the room. It was clear that Skye was not well-liked. "Tomorrow we will go over expectations for the band room. Now—could I hear the trumpets at measure thirty-three?"

It would be a very long semester.

·········

Millie knocked on the door to Tabitha's office. "Ready to eat?"

Tabitha shut her computer down. "Is it already time? Let's go; I'm hungry."

"You didn't bring your lunch?"

"No. I understood that lunches were free to teachers. Do most of you bring your lunch? They do serve lunch, right?"

"You can decide for yourself," said Millie, waggling her eyebrows. She spotted Tabitha's purse on top of a file cabinet. "If you're not taking your purse, lock your office door."

"Surely I don't need to—"

"Would you leave your purse unattended at Walmart? This is public school." Millie waited while Tabitha locked her door.

Once Tabitha had her tray she found Millie, and whispered, "Who is that older woman with the orange hair in the lunch line?"

"That's Miss Libby. Libby Lancaster, but everyone knows her as Libby the Librarian, or just Miss Libby. Have you met?'

"No, but I saw her this morning in the office and wondered about her."

"She's great. She's got a heart of gold. She's been here forever and doesn't take crap from anyone—just does whatever the spirit moves her to do. That woman does not care. She's my idol." Millie nudged Tabitha and pointed to the huge, red plastic buffet the lunch ladies were serving from. "Watch."

Miss Libby nonchalantly inched her way to the lunch ladies' side.

Millie whispered in Tabitha's ear, "See that little boy in line, the one in the yellow hoodie? He won't eat anything but fruit, but students are only allowed one serving."

Tabitha looked at her plate of nachos and baked French fries. *A couple of pieces of fruit are sounding pretty good about now.*

Miss Libby and a heavyset lunch lady seemed to be in a scuffle for the fruit salad ladle. Miss Libby was strong and wiry, but the lunch lady was definitely broader in the beam and hip-bumped her out of her way. Libby walked away, seemingly defeated, but Tabitha saw her pull an apple and an orange from her pockets and deposit it on the boy's tray as she passed by.

"She will do anything for the good of a child, and she doesn't care about anything else. That is what I aspire to when I am old."

A few minutes later the high school students came roaring into the cafeteria.

"Tell me about Skye," said Tabitha.

"Skye. Hmm. There's so much to tell, and yet so little. Skye and her mother showed up in Medicine Creek last summer. No one knows much about them. They live on the outskirts of town in a trailer park. The mother doesn't work, as far as I know. In any case, Skye keeps to herself. She hasn't adjusted well to small-town life and hasn't made any friends. She's in band, as you know, and she showed up for all the football games and performances, but her mother never showed any support. I think the previous band director took her under her wing, and when she disappeared Skye took it hard and shut down. She walks several miles to school and is never late, so that says something, and she has a job, as you know. Most of the town considers her a transient, and I'm afraid that's how quite a few teachers view her, so they don't make any real effort to involve her. It's sad."

Tabitha watched as Skye slunk in. She stood in the lunch line, alone and hunched over, black hoodie pulled low over her face, looking for all the world like she didn't need anyone. Tabitha found it hard to reconcile this version with the one that swaggered into the band room, or the mouthy girl Tabitha met at the Sweet Shoppe, and despite what Millie said, Skye *was* late this morning. Tabitha nibbled at a limp french fry, watching her. All around, teenagers joked and smiled, sure of their place in the world. *Maybe it's not that Skye doesn't need anyone; maybe no one needs Skye.* She dipped her fry in ketchup and tried one more bite before giving up. *I am going to start bringing my lunch.*

"You know what, Millie? Skye's luck is about to change."

Their eyes met. "I hope so, Tabitha. I really do."

Chapter 13
Pain All Around

The last bell rang. As soon as the last student left the band room Tabitha dropped her head, exhausted. Someone cleared their throat. Tabitha raised her head to see her new principal, Mr. Roundtree, hovering in the doorway.

"So you made it through your first day," he said. "Good job."

Tabitha ran a hand through her hair. "I thought the first graders might have done me in for a minute, but we got through together."

"It's not like that fancy school you came from, is it?"

She grinned. "Not in the least."

"I knew you'd like this better. Not those snooty rich kids you taught before. Just good ol' regular kids here."

Tabitha frowned, unsure how to respond, deciding silence was her best course. She gathered some stray papers into a neat stack before looking up to find Mr. Roundtree staring at her through his thick glasses—or at least she thought he was.

He cleared his throat again. "Well, if there's anything you need—anything at all—just let me know. My door is always open. See you tomorrow."

"Well, there is something that would be nice to have."

The principal blinked, not expecting this. "Yes?"

"I can't find any rhythm instruments for the younger grades."

Mr. Roundtree blinked again. "Rhythm instruments?"

"Yes, maybe some hand drums, a few tambor—"

"Miss Reed didn't use those." Blink, blink.

"The teacher that left?"

Neither blinked this time. Mr. Roundtree cleared his throat, but Tabitha pushed on before he could speak. "I understand, but I've used them before and they are great teaching tools..."

The principal's eyes narrowed. "So you think you have to have them."

Outside, a car honked. Children's muffled laughter drifted in. A Bird chirped. Tabitha did not break eye contact. He scratched his nose and hitched his pants up over his ample belly.

"I'll see what I can do."

"Thank you." *Goodness, did I just win?*

He turned and lumbered down the hall, muttering to himself as Tabitha strained to hear. Her eyes opened wide.

Did he just call me Miss Fancy-Pants?

Standing at the edge of the back parking lot, Tabitha looked for Gran's Buick. *Did Nick park in the front? I told him to come to the teacher's parking lot.* Tabitha hoisted her backpack higher on her shoulder and headed around the building. A horn blasted in the lot. She looked back but kept walking. An old truck pulled out of a parking place and crept along behind her. *Is that the man who gave me the ride to the laundromat?* She studied the way the grass pushed through the cracked sidewalk, not wanting to make eye contact, and increased her pace—not so much that she looked afraid, but enough to show purpose, she hoped. Whoever it was, they were rolling down their window.

"Get in," said Nick. *Nick.* She released air noisily, not realizing she was holding her breath.

Tabitha set her backpack on the floorboard. "I didn't recognize you. Is this old truck yours?"

"This old truck is a vintage '63 Chevy C-10 with original Glenwood Green paint. And yes, it belongs to me."

"It's pretty."

Nick rolled his eyes.

"Would you mind if we stop at The Sweet Shoppe? You know—kind of celebrate my first day?"

Nick gave her a quick side-eye. "I do not have much time, but yes, we can do that."

By the time Tabitha and Nick got there, the shop was packed with students holding cookies and steaming cups of hot chocolate. Tabitha tapped the corner of her mouth as she looked for Skye. "She's not here."

"Who?"

"Skye." Tabitha dropped her hand.

"Is that the emo girl?"

"Yes."

Nick pointed over her head, toward the kitchen. "She is in the back."

Tabitha pointed toward the empty table. "Do you have time to sit down?"

Nick checked his phone. "I have fifteen minutes. You came here to talk to that girl. Go sit down. I will order. Do you want coffee?"

"Hot cocoa, please."

"Got it."

"And a sugar cookie."

"Got it."

Tabitha tapped her lip. "The one on the left with pink icing."

Nick didn't move, yet somehow conveyed to Tabitha that she should probably stop talking and find a seat.

About halfway through her cookie, Tabitha caught Skye's attention and waved her over.

"How are you?"

"Fine. Do you need something?"

"No, I just wanted to say hi. I was glad to see you in band today, even if you were a smidge late."

Skye turned her attention to Nick. "Do you need anything?" Nick shook his head no. "So. This was fun."

Tabitha tapped her chin, then flapped her hand at Skye before she could leave.

It's cool that you play flute. That's my principal instrument. If you need any help—"

"I don't."

"Well, just know that if you change your mind, I am a pro and would love to help you." Tabitha touched Skye's arm. She jerked away as if Tabitha's touch burned, her face full of malice.

"Let me get this straight. You are a professional flute player, but you came here—to Medicine Creek—to teach in this podunk town. Do you think you're going to get discovered here?"

Tabitha's cheeks flamed. "No, I, uh..."

"Those who can, do. Those who can't—teach public school in the middle of nowhere. Leave me alone." Skye walked away before Tabitha could reply.

Nick scooted his chair back. "We have to get going."

Nick put the truck in reverse before Tabitha could collect herself enough to talk. "I did not expect that." She paused, waiting for Nick to commiserate with her. Nothing. "I can't believe that she thinks teaching means I'm not at a professional level."

"Are you?" Nick kept his eyes on the road.

"Am I what?"

"At a professional level?"

Oh my god, I can't believe this. "I am. Why is that so hard to believe?" Nick shrugged. "As a matter of fact, I have an audition coming up with a very prestigious chamber group." *The group I'm not auditioning for.*

"I am not judging you; I have never heard you play. That sort of thing takes dedication." He could see Tabitha's shoulders relax.

"It does. I've dedicated most of my life to music."

"So when is the audition?"

"January twelfth." Tabitha leaned her head against the window and sighed. Once the sun set, the temperature dropped dramatically, and a few snowflakes drifted down. The heater in Nick's truck didn't work well and once again she wished she had her scarf.

Nick pulled into the drive. "Tell Gran I will be home around seven."

⋯•••••••⋯

The conversations, first with Skye, then with Nick, depressed her. Tabitha sat by her window with a cup of hot tea and watched the snowflakes drift over the river. She dialed Zamarri's number.

"Helloo?" Tabitha loved Zamarri's accent. A welcome wave of familiarity washed over her and it comforted her to hear her old friend's voice and talk music. Serious artists like Zamarri and Miki would understand.

"Tabitha! It is so good to hear your voice. I have not heard from you but did not want to call. I know you are practicing and didn't want to disturb you. How are you?"

"Good, good. I'm just checking in." Tabitha told her about the exchange with Skye.

Zamarri exploded with indignation. "This student does not know the sacrifices we make for our art. But don't be upset, because you'll ace the audition and will no longer have any need to teach at the Academy."

Oh my god, I didn't tell her I quit.

"Strike her from your mind. You and I will be in Paris this summer. And I just learned we are invited to play in Edinburgh at the Fringe. I'll be in New York in May for a brief break. Meet me there and we can fly to Paris together. The audition is so close. You are prepared?"

Tabitha closed her eyes. "Zamarri, I can't make the audition."

"What? Of course you can. You have been preparing for months. Don't speak nonsense."

"Zamarri, you know a lot has been going on, what with the divorce and all."

"Of course I know this. Now Michael is out of your life, and good riddance to him. It is time to focus on yourself." She paused. "You have been practicing?"

"Well, not as much as I'd hoped. Michael kicked me out and I had to find a new job—"

Zamarri cut in. "You have a new job?"

"Yes, and with the move and everything..."

'You know what, Tabitha? I am done. I told you not to marry the fool, to put your music first, but you would not listen. There is always an excuse with you."

"I had responsibilities—"

"And they are gone so you make yourself new ones. This Skye is correct. Going pro is a dream to you, not a goal. Teaching is noble, but you have the talent that others long for. You choose good when you could choose best. You're afraid of taking risks, and that is what life is all about. Good luck, Tabitha."

Tabitha stared at her phone, tears trickling down her cheeks. She punched in her mother's number but hung up before it rang. A cold draft snaked its way in under the window sill. She shivered but didn't move. Zamarri didn't understand. She had grown up in France with parents who valued art above all. Zamarri's parents had always made her feel she was the most precious thing on earth, and encouraged her every step.

She didn't know the pain of growing up with a mother who didn't understand, who thought music was nothing more than a pleasant hobby, and who believed teaching was the only sensible, viable career choice. A vehicle turned in the drive, its headlights reflecting the blowing snow. Tabitha washed her face and headed downstairs. Now that Nick was home they would eat soon.

It startled her to see Atticus in the foyer instead of Nick, his hat in hand, his expression all business.

"What's going on?" she asked, looking from Gran to Atticus.

"He won't say until Nick gets here." Gran turned to Atticus. "Are you sure you don't want to take your coat off and stay for dinner?"

"No thank you," he said, his face inscrutable.

Nick's truck pulled in beside the patrol car. A moment later Nick entered, stomping snow from his boots, the two men eyeing each other all the while. Gran could feel the energy between them and didn't like it.

"We have identified the body, " Atticus looked Nick square in the eye. "It was Claire."

Nick sucked in air. "You are sure?"

"Yes."

"How did she die?"

"Homicide. I can't say more right now."

Gran's hand flew to her mouth.

"I wanted to tell you first—before word gets out."

"Well, you told me," Nick said, his face hard.

Atticus put his hat on and adjusted the brim. He opened the door. "I'm sorry," he said, his back to everyone. The screen door slammed behind him.

"Gran, I believe I will turn in for the night."

Gran hugged him. "I'll make a plate, just in case you get hungry later." She watched him go up the stairs, then patted Tabitha's arm. "Let's you and I have a little dinner." She noticed Tabitha's red eyes but said nothing.

"Gran?"

"Yes, honey?"

"Who was Claire? She was someone special to Nick?"

Gran handed Tabitha a bowl of mashed potatoes, waiting to speak until their plates were filled.

"Claire Reed. The music teacher. The band director." Tabitha looked at her with enormous eyes. "Everyone said the town ran her off, but Nick never believed it. He knew something bad happened to her."

·········

There was no slice of light under Nick's door when Tabitha entered the bathroom to shower. She let the hot water beat down on her, dissolving the tension between her shoulders as she contemplated the latest events in town. As she rinsed the conditioner from her hair, Tabitha wondered if Skye had heard. *Probably. News travels fast here. How is she taking it?* A few minutes later Tabitha drifted into an uneasy sleep.

Chapter 14

Rumors

The next morning the school buzzed with the news. Tabitha found Millie as she walked toward the lunchroom.

"I see you brought your lunch," Millie joked.

Tabitha laughed. "I learned my lesson." The two sat at the teacher table, their backs to the mayhem that was the cafeteria.

"So, how is Skye doing?" Millie asked between bites.

Tabitha shrugged. "She was absent. At least for my class." Tabitha unwrapped the sandwich she'd made that morning.

"Ooh." Millie grimaced. "That's not going to help her case."

"Her case?" Tabitha's brows puckered.

"The rumors are flying. First Vinnie, then Miss Reed."

"How do they have anything to do with Skye?" Tabitha asked.

"Unbeknownst to me, Skye's mother and Vinnie were, um, friends, you might say." Millie took a gulp of water.

"Romantically?"

"More like partners in crime. People say they were druggies. Whether true or not, they definitely hung out on the bad side of town."

"I didn't know there was a bad side of town."

"Oh, there is. South of the laundromat it's a whole other world. Oak Street—the street that runs from Gran's to the laundromat—is the dividing line." Millie shook the crumbs from her bag of chips into her mouth. "That's where Skye lives. That's where the public housing is. And the liquor store. The good people of Medicine Creek do not want their 'unfortunates' out in public view."

"I still don't see a connection to Skye, other than her liking her teacher."

High school students filled the cafeteria, and Libby the Librarian pushed her way to the front of the line. Today she wore lime-green leggings, a silver-sequined top with the shoulders cut out, and enormous rhinestone earrings that brushed the top of her bare shoulders. She spotted Millie and Tabitha, and as soon as she got her tray, made a bee-line over to them.

"Well, I guess you heard the news," she said, plopping down beside them. Millie's lips tightened and she shook her head at Tabitha imperceptibly.

"Yes. Tragic," said Millie.

"Tragic? I don't know that I'd call it tragic, but it's definitely interesting," Libby nodded sagely.

"What's interesting?" Tabitha couldn't help herself despite Millie's warning.

Libby beamed. "I heard that Skye's mom wasn't home last night, and no one's seen her." She shoveled in a spoonful of mixed veggies drenched in pretend butter.

"And Skye wasn't in class," Tabitha mused. The three women looked at one another, Libby's mouth still full. She chewed and swallowed.

"Rumor has it that her mother is a suspect." Libby's eyes sparkled. "And everyone knows that Miss Reed and Nick fought right before her disappearance."

Millie gathered her lunch bag. "Well, girls, it's been fun. I'm supposed to tell you there's a faculty meeting after school, and there's never any telling how long it will go. Would you like a ride home?"

"That'd be great. I'll let Nick know I've got a ride."

"See you later."

"Bye." Tabitha looked at the clock. There were still seven more minutes before class. "I hope we didn't upset her."

"Don't worry about Millie. She loves gossip but is careful to appear above it all, which is smart. She's *somebody* and doesn't like to get 'involved'."

"You think Skye's mother is a suspect?"

"Atticus showed up at her trailer last night and she didn't come to the door."

"Where did you hear that?"

"Agnes told me."

"Agnes?"

"Yeah. You met her."

"I don't think so."

"Yes, you did. Tiny little thing. You two found Vinnie at the laundry mat."

Oh, that Agnes. "Yes. Sorry. Now I remember. So how does Agnes figure into all this?"

"Agnes is my baby sister. She lives next door to Skye and her mother. Agnes said Atticus banged and banged on the door but no one answered."

"Maybe she was out of town."

Libby raised her eyebrows and an army of wrinkles marched across her forehead. "Skye's mom doesn't have a vehicle, so if she left town, someone had to help her." She could see Tabitha's intrigue and winked. "I could find out."

"How?" Tabitha knew she should leave this alone but couldn't help herself.

"I have my ways." Libby waggled her brows.

Tabitha shook her head. "No, this is crazy. This is not the kind of thing we should be involved in."

"Suit yourself." Libby eased her legs from under the table and patted Tabitha on the shoulder. "Have a good day."

....

Mr. Roundtree tapped on a library table. "Good afternoon. Welcome to our January faculty meeting. I think everyone is here, so let's get started." He cleared his throat. "I am sure you have heard the rumors flying around. I would remind you that you are professionals, and that gossip is beneath you."

"Especially since we already know." A heavy-set man in tight athletic shorts leaned back in his chair, his shirt hiked up over his large, hairy stomach. The man looked around, grinning at no one in particular, his gaze settling on Mr. Roundtree. Tabitha noticed her new boss's jaw tighten, but he refrained from commenting.

"Who is that?" Tabitha whispered in Millie's ear. Millie rolled her eyes.

"That's Coach Randall. He thinks he's god's gift to women. And to the world in general. He invested in the pot farm when it opened and acts like he's a millionaire. The farther away you stay from him the better."

"He creeps me out." Tabitha shuddered.

"He creeps everyone out. He's always lurking around, trying to hit on anyone he can, saying inappropriate things, but Roundtree never says a thing to him."

"I wonder what secret Mr. Roundtree has that Coach Randall knows about?" Tabitha winked at Millie, then glanced at Coach Randall. He winked. *Augh. Surely he didn't think I was winking at him?*

Mr. Roundtree continued. "Just a reminder that last month a sign-up sheet went around for food items for the Winter Carnival. I expect everyone to bring something. The raffle and the cake-walk are our biggest money-makers, as you know, so let's make it good."

"Winter Carnival? When is that?" Tabitha whispered.

"Tomorrow night. The whole town shows up. It's a lot of work, so you're lucky you didn't have to man a booth this time. We're expected to donate baked goods for the auction and buy tickets to the raffle. It's a wonderful prize this year. Martial arts lessons. I happen to be selling them." Millie fluttered her lashes.

Tabitha rustled inside her purse. "Here. I'll buy fifty dollars' worth to support the cause, but you will never see me inside a dojo or anyplace else that requires exertion. I sit. I read. I play music. But I do not, under any condition, sweat."

·········

Millie waited for the Sheriff's Ranger to back out of Gran's drive so she could drop Tabitha off. She looked at Tabitha, curious, but said nothing. Tabitha could hear Nick's voice before she even got inside. She opened the front door and stood in the foyer, unsure of what to do.

"You heard him; he knew where she was going and did nothing to stop her. And now she is dead. He could have done something. He could have protected her."

Tabitha stopped on the porch; she'd never heard Nick raise his voice. Gran said something but she couldn't make it out.

"He could have told me. I would have stopped her. But he did not tell me, and now Claire is gone." Nick stormed up the stairs.

Tabitha tapped on the door frame. "Is everything okay? I saw Atticus's vehicle pull away."

"I'm afraid everything is not okay, but come in. I'll make a pot of tea." Gran smiled, but her heart wasn't in it. Once the tea steeped, Gran patted the table. "Sit."

"I assume Nick and Miss Reed were seeing each other? Was it serious?"

Gran sipped her tea. "It was well on its way. He was extremely fond of her. Nick sticks to himself—always has. Claire brought out something in him he doesn't show many people. And now this." Whatever Atticus had said, it had extinguished Gran's spark.

"Why was Atticus here?"

"He came by to tell Nick they discovered her body by the river. I feel like there's more but he's holding back." Gran rubbed the back of her neck. "I better go work on dinner."

"How about we just get take-out? We're all emotionally exhausted."

Gran smiled. "That's sweet, but cooking grounds me. And I already made a pot of potato soup. I just have to make a salad."

After dinner, Tabitha remembered the dessert she had to bring for the Winter Carnival.

"Gran, would you mind taking me to the grocery store? There's a school carnival tomorrow and I need to buy a dessert for the auction."

Gran's brows shot up. "Tabby, you can not bring store-bought to the Winter Carnival."

"I just found out about it this afternoon, and I have no kitchen. People will understand."

Nick's cheek twitched as he looked at Gran. *Is he laughing?*

"No, honey, they will not understand. I will make something tomorrow while you're a work, and your reputation will remain intact. Besides, everyone knows you stay here. Both of our reputations would be tarnished." Gran opened her eyes wide, pretending shock.

"Thank you. I wouldn't want to ruin us both my first week."

· · · · • · • · · · ·

The whole town turned out for the Winter Carnival, and once Tabitha saw the stage lined from end-to-end with homemade deliciousness, she silently thanked Gran for keeping her from bringing a store-bought cake. Tabitha was stunned that Gran's poppy-seed cake sold for two hundred dollars.

Tabitha and Millie had just finished serving cookies and punch when the raffle began. Millie grabbed Tabitha's wrist and pulled her toward the stage. "Come on. Let's see who wins. Everyone bought raffle tickets this time." said Millie, giving Tabitha a wink.

"Why? What's being raffled?"

"Twenty-five private martial arts lessons. I think everybody in town bought one."

"Well, I hope I don't win. That sounds like twenty-five lessons from hell."

"Yeah, sure. That's why you bought fifty tickets," Millie smirked. "You know he's hot, you lucky thing."

"What? Who is hot?" Tabitha asked.

At that moment Mr. Roundtree waddled up to the podium, leaned into the mic, and cleared his throat. "Could I have your attention, please? I hope everyone is enjoying our Winter Carnival. We'll begin with this beautiful quilt made by Mrs.

Beverly Binks. Isn't it lovely?" Friendly bickering echoed off the cafeteria walls as each item was auctioned off.

"Now I would like to draw the winner for the raffle. This year Spotted Wolf Dojo has made an extremely generous donation of twenty-five private martial arts lessons—a $750 value! And the lucky winner is..." He reached into a large glass bowl and pulled out a ticket. "Ticket number 181236." He looked around expectantly but no one claimed it. "Please check your tickets for number 181236."

Libby, in a long orange dress with pink paper flowers in her hair, made her way to where Millie and Tabitha were. Tabitha stared in consternation at her ticket while Millie, peering over her shoulder, chortled. "Right here! Ms. Peterson won. Come on, Tabitha, go up and claim your prize."

"Woo-hoo! Lucky you. That boy is hot." Libby shouted, grinning lasciviously.

"Who is hot?" Tabitha asked Millie under her breath. Millie rolled her eyes. "Sure. You never noticed."

Tabitha climbed the steps to the stage, where Mr. Roundtree waited. On the far side of the stage, Nick took the steps two at a time. *Nick?* Mr. Roundtree clapped her on the back as Nick held out the gift certificate, *Spotted Wolf Dojo* printed across the top in gold. Tabitha's jaw dropped. Nick bent down to shake her hand and hand her the certificate, whispering, "Close your mouth." Tabitha's mouth snapped shut but her eyes remained wide open. *Nick teaches martial arts? Oh my gosh, he is hot. How did I miss that? And I'm expected to take private lessons—in a room alone with him?*

Chapter 15

Dead Composers

When is this carnival going to be over? I need a break. Tabitha eased her way toward the cafeteria exit and into the deserted hallway leading to the band room. Halfway down the darkened hall, a strong hand gripped her upper arm and Tabitha yelped.

"Where are you going?" Coach Randall showed his teeth.

Is that his smile? "I just needed a little air. It's hot in the cafeteria." Tabitha stared pointedly at her arm until he released her.

"We haven't met, have we? I'm Coach Randall, and you must be the new band director. The girl before you was attractive in an athletic sort of way, but you're as cute as a bug, like a little lap dog. Miss Peterson, correct?"

"Ms. Peterson. Millie pointed you out during the faculty meeting."

"Oh she did, did she?" More teeth.

"Yes." Tabitha made her voice as cold as she could. "She pointed everyone out. Now if you'll excuse me." She tried to brush past him but he shifted and stood in her path.

"Why such a hurry?"

"I have a phone call to make. I have to check in with Michael. My husband." *Why did that come out of my mouth?*

"Oh. I didn't know you were married."

"No, you would not." Tabitha walked down the hall as fast as she could without looking like she was running away.

Once in the band room, she locked the door. She sat on the rickety wooden piano bench, her back to the keyboard. She looked around absently, noting the carpet stained from years of emptying water valves, and faded, splotchy beige paint. *I wonder if Roundtree would spring for paint if I offered to do it myself?*

She pivoted to face the piano and played a few notes. *It's in better tune than I expected.* She relaxed and began a Chopin prelude that matched her mood. After the last note, she sighed and pulled the fallboard over the keys. A piece of staff paper on top of the old upright fluttered to the floor and Tabitha picked it up. Someone had scribbled down a bit of music in pencil. *A. Reed* was printed neatly in the upper-right-hand corner. The piece, titled, *I'm Not...* was little more than a three-note motif, repeated over and over. *I guess this is a student's, but whose? I don't remember an A. Reed. Do I have an A. Reed in class?* She went into her office and scrolled through her roster. No one named Reed. *Oh well. At least a student is trying to compose. That's something. I'll ask tomorrow.* Tabitha turned off the light and sat in the dark, hoping Coach Randall had decided to lurk elsewhere. Her phone buzzed. It was a text from Millie:

> Where are you?
>
> I'm in the band room, hiding from Coach Randall. Come rescue me.
>
> I'll be right there.

"Tabitha?" Millie tapped on the door. "Why are you sitting in the dark?"

"Trying to trick Coach Randall into thinking I'm not here. Did it work?" Tabitha peered out the door.

"I guess so; at least I didn't see him. I told you he was a creeper. Did he do something?"

"No, he just startled me. I'm fine. It's been a long day, and with these murders, I'm a little on edge."

"I think everyone is." Millie tucked her arm in Tabitha's. "Well, the carnival is winding down. Let's go say our goodbyes and get out of here. Tomorrow morning is going to be here soon enough."

"Hey, Millie, did you see Skye tonight?"

"No. I heard she and her mother skipped town."

"Why?" Tabitha stopped walking.

Millie took her arm. "Tabitha, everyone says Skye's mom and Vinnie were close. They could have been friends or lovers or just junkie buddies." She lowered her voice. "The word is that Skye and her mother might be involved with the murders somehow, but you didn't hear that from me."

"I don't believe it."

'Hon, I know you like the girl, but you don't know her like we do. That family is bad news. If they left, it's sad, but it's for the best."

"I don't believe she's bad. She's a child. I hope she's here tomorrow. Maybe I can help her."

"You have a good heart, Tabitha Peterson. It's better not to get personally involved, though."

Tabitha's jaw set. "We'll see."

"It's a carnival; let's go have some fun." Millie grinned and flapped her hands like a five-year-old, making Tabitha laugh as they entered the cafeteria.

Farther down the darkened hall, Coach Randall stood in the shadow close to the wall, watching.

"You need to get this heater fixed. Your truck is freezing," Tabitha said, pulling her coat lapel up to her chin. "I didn't know you taught martial arts."

"You did not ask."

Tabitha rolled her eyes. "So what kind of martial arts do you do?"

"Tae-kwon-do is the most popular, but I like aikido and judo best. That is what I will teach you."

"Oh, about that—"

Nick slammed on his brakes, his arm shooting out across Tabitha's chest as something streaked across the road. "You okay?" he asked, his arm still out.

"Yes. What was that?"

"Bobcat."

"A bobcat? Wow. I had no idea bobcats were around here." Tabitha gently pushed his arm down.

"Sorry. Instinct."

"I didn't know you had such fast reflexes."

"I have many talents you are unaware of."

Tabitha was suddenly glad for the dark.

·········

River sat first-chair and was serious about keeping it. Tabitha, still in her office, could hear her warming up. The girl was dedicated.

"River, have you ever auditioned for All-State?" Tabitha called through the open door.

"What?"

"I said, have you ever auditioned for All-State?" Tabitha found the score she needed and came out of her office but froze in the doorway. River had the scarf Tabitha's mother had knitted wound around her neck. The one Skye had taken. "Where did you get that scarf?"

River set her flute on her knee. "I don't remember. I think my mother got it for me. Oh yeah. I got it for Christmas. She ordered it online," she said, not making eye contact.

The other kids were trickling in. "You know, let's just wait so I can tell everyone," said Tabitha. *How did she get my scarf, and why is she lying about it?*

·········

Tabitha touched Millie's arm as they entered the cafeteria. "Millie, we have to talk. Privately," Tabitha whispered.

Millie's gaze darted around the room. "I don't see any bad guys. I think we're okay."

"I mean it. Let me get a tray first."

Tabitha sat down beside Millie and looked at her food. "What is this?" She poked at the concoction with her fork.

"Ooh, we call that po-tachos, a local delicacy. Chopped up tater-tots, baked and drenched with liquid cheese sauce mixed with a delicious mystery meat, then covered in jalapenos and salt. Why didn't you bring your lunch?"

"No time. Anyway, we need to talk. Someone left sheet music on my piano."

"Oh no!" Millie's hand flew to her mouth, her eyes twinkling.

"Funny. But there's more. River has Skye's scarf."

"How do you know it's Skye's scarf?

"Because my mother made it."

"Your mother made Skye a scarf?"

"No," said Tabitha, exasperated. "It's mine."

"You told me you lost it."

"That's not the point."

"You lied to me?"

"What did she lie to you about?" Both women looked up to see Libby loping over. Today she wore a red jersey dress with deep orange gores, hot-pink stilettos, and a gigantic pink plastic geometric necklace.

"Oh my god, will you both hush?" Tabitha almost yelled.

"We don't say—" they both began.

"I know. *I know.* You two are exhausting. Look, we can't talk here. Meet me in the band room after school."

Millie shook her head. "I'm not sure I can."

"Well, wild horses couldn't keep me away," said Libby, waggling her entire upper torso.

"After school," Tabitha said. Libby shot her a thumbs-up. They both looked at Millie.

She shook her head. "*Fine.* But five minutes, then I'm gone."

·····●·●····

The last bell rang. Tabitha sat down at the piano while she waited for Millie and Libby. She noodled around, then picked up the sheet music she'd found yesterday. Today another piece rested underneath. *What is going on?*

This piece was also titled, *I'm Not... by A. Reed*. Tabitha played it. This time it was a four-note motif. Neither was developed at all, just a simple motif repeated—one in 3/4 and the new one in 4/4. Tabitha played the new one over and over, then pulled the first one out and played it a few times, too engrossed to notice Millie and Libby come in.

"What are you playing?" asked Libby. "I don't know much about music, and no offense, but it's not very catchy."

"It's not, is it?" Tabitha agreed. Libby lowered herself to the bench beside Tabitha.

"How do you read music? I never could figure out how to read music."

"It's easy. The lines are *Every Good Boy Deserves Fudge* and the spaces between spell *F-A-C-E*. Understand?"

"Yeah, the understanding is easy. It's the remembering that's hard."

"Let me explain a different way; see that little line below the staff? That's 'C', then you just say the alphabet up to 'B', then start over. So... 'A B C D E F G'. That's all there is to it. You just keep practicing, and then—voila!"

"Voila!" Libby repeated in a heavy accent. "Voila!"

Millie interjected. "So what is this secret meeting about?"

"Skye either gave my scarf away or someone took it from her," said Tabitha.

"Or she dropped it, or—well, anything. I don't see that this is a big deal." Millie looked at Libby for support but Libby had her nose in the music.

"It could mean that Skye is still in town."

"So what? Tabitha, you're a teacher, not a detective. Let Atticus handle it."

"Millie, there are two unsolved murders. *Unsolved*. That means the murderer is still out there. And there is a young girl that no one can locate. Doesn't that worry you?"

"It worries me enough to not go poking around."

Tabitha shook her head. "Why doesn't anyone care about Skye? I think it's at least worth going to her house to see if she's still there."

"It's not that I don't care about her, but how does it matter whether she's moved away or skipping school?" asked Millie, her voice rising.

"Hush," said Tabitha, walking over to close the band room door. Libby, in deep concentration, ignored them both.

"I need to know. If you don't want to help me, I get it, but I need to know," said Tabitha.

"I wish I could, but I can't get involved. And you shouldn't either. Look, I can't do this. I'm sorry."

Tabitha leaned her head against the piano, dejected. "Libby, what do you think?"

"I'm not bad!" Libby chortled. "Voila!"

"What?" Tabitha peeked under her arm at Libby, who was grinning like she won the lottery.

"It's the song! B-A-D, those are the right notes, aren't they? *I'm Not... Bad!*"

Tabitha bolted upright and snatched the staff paper from the piano. She studied the first song, then the second. D-E-A-D. "And *I'm Not... Dead*! They're messages! Libby, I could kiss you!"

Chapter 16
The Hunt Is On

Libby parked behind the laundromat. She perched on the hood of her Cadillac, dressed in a shiny black spandex bodysuit, her red hair tucked into a black stocking cap, a cheap black satin cape draped over her thin shoulders. Her long, bony arms and legs poked out where the body suit should have met her gloves and boots, and she'd smudged something black on each cheek. Tabitha, in jeans and a hoodie, rounded the corner and stopped short, taking it all in.

"Pretty cool, huh?" Libby's dentures gleamed in the light of the single street lamp, red curls poking out erratically around the edge of the cap. Libby twirled, the cape flapping around her. She stuck an arm out to steady herself, dizzy. "Stealth-mode. We don't want anyone noticing us."

"Right."

Libby gave Tabitha the once over, her disappointment in Tabitha's choice of attire apparent.

"It's okay. You can be the normal person, and I can do all the sleuthing." Libby looked as if she might spin again and Tabitha grabbed her arm.

"No more twirling. I'm cold, let's get in the car." Tabitha hoped no one had seen Libby's get-up. "You know where Skye lives?"

"Yep. Right next door to Agnes. She loaned me this cool bodysuit but she needs it back by Friday."

Tabitha closed her eyes, trying hard not to wonder why Agnes had to have the bodysuit back.

"She's a dancer, but she's off until Saturday. Pulled her hamstring."

"Dancing?" Tabitha asked, incredulous.

Libby waggled her eyebrows and giggled. "Nope."

Tabitha swung her head to look at Libby as visions of Agnes prancing around a stage in spandex flooded into her brain. *I will never be able to erase these images.*

"Let's go." Tabitha buckled her seat belt as Libby pulled out. "Your headlights aren't on."

"Stealth-mode."

"I don't think we need to be that stealthy. I don't want to die."

"Have it your way." Libby turned the headlights on and drove south. After a few miles, the road turned from asphalt to gravel, then dirt. The houses were fewer and farther between, with most not taken care of in any meaningful way.

"Your sister lives out here?"

"Yep. This is where we grew up. The old stompin' grounds."

The street lights ended with the gravel, and clouds had blown in, obscuring the moon. An old red truck passed by, heading into town, its cab light on. Tabitha could see two men inside but couldn't make out who they were before the cab light went off. Something seemed familiar, but Tabitha couldn't decide if it was the truck or its occupants.

"Did you see who was in that truck?"

"Nope, but it belongs to Ned Ryan."

"What does Ned do for a living?"

"He used to work for the Blackhorns, but I heard he got let go for doing something nefarious. It was too bad because that's a good job. The Blackhorns take care of their employees, and Ned has a family. Now I heard he works at that new pot farm, the Happy Haze."

"Did you recognize his passenger? I feel like I've seen him before. A big guy wearing an orange ball cap."

Libby chuckled. "That's not much to go on. The men grow big around here, and everybody wears ball caps." She slowed down and scanned the side of the road to her right, then pulled over and turned the headlights off.

"What are you doing?"

"Something's wrong." Libby chewed on a fingernail, eyes narrowed, focused on something far away. "Do you see a light up there?" She pointed into the darkness. "Three o'clock, at the top of the tree line."

"I don't see anything. It's pitch dark out here." Tabitha kept looking, just in case.

"Yeah, I guess you're right. Sure thought I saw something flickering at the top of the hill for a hot second." She eased back onto the road. A half-mile later she pulled into what could only loosely be called a trailer park. It looked to Tabitha as if a few ramshackle trailers had been dumped in a field and tied together by a slew of crisscrossing electrical lines. Libby pulled up to a small trailer lit up with an insane amount of Christmas lights.

"That's Agnes's place," she said proudly. "And that one next to her is where Skye and Bonnie—her mother—live." Tabitha studied it curiously and decided it looked creepy and uninhabited. Libby flashed her lights twice before she cut the engine and the two women opened the car doors. Agnes's front door opened. Light spilled out, silhouetting a small, dark figure holding an extremely large rifle.

"Are you positive this is the right place?" Tabitha asked.

"Are you crazy? I know my own sister. Don't you recognize her from the laundromat?"

Agnes moved to the side of the door, and now hundreds of Christmas lights cast a rosy glow over her neon-green and orange muumuu, stovepipe hat, and fuzzy yellow slippers. At least she'd lowered the rifle.

"Maybe we should stay in the car. That's a big rifle," said Tabitha.

"It's fine. I flashed twice. Looks like she's been cleaning." Tabitha didn't ask.

"Come on in, it's cold out here," Agnes yelled. Libby climbed the porch steps. Standing next to each other, Tabitha could see the family resemblance, though Libby had a good ten inches on her sister. Once inside, Tabitha stopped cold. A hot-pink velvet sofa took up an entire wall, while an enormous wooden pony painted silver and purple stood guard in the center of the room, presumably from a defunct merry-go-round. There were mirrors everywhere—hung on walls and perched on shelves, but the coup de grace was a giant gilded floor mirror propped against the kitchen wall. It reminded Tabitha of something that might have hung in a grand opera house. Or a brothel.

"It's a demented fun-house," Tabitha blurted out, then slapped her hand over her mouth.

"I know, right? I decorated it myself. Make yourself comfortable." Agnes gestured grandly. "Want a coke? I hardly ever have guests." Agnes stuck her head in her refrigerator. "And I have milk if it's not curdled," she called out, her voice muffled..

Tabitha began to put her arm on the pony's back but Libby slapped it away, violently shaking her head. "You don't want to touch that," she whispered, eyes wide and knowing. "That's where she pulled her hamstring."

Tabitha jumped away, horrified. "Too much information."

Tabitha pulled herself together as Agnes handed her a pop. "Agnes, have you seen Skye lately?"

"No. It's been real quiet over there the last few days."

"Have you seen her mother?"

"Bonnie? Nope. Not since Vinnie's... demise." Agnes looked pleased with herself. "Do you know what *demise* means?" She looked at Tabitha.

"Yes. Yes I do. Are you saying Bonnie and Vinnie knew each other?"

"Sure. They worked together at Happy Haze. Those two were thick as thieves. He was always in and out over there. Well, up until Bonnie caught him with that music teacher, but it was weird because I thought Bonnie was sweet on some other guy."

"The *music* teacher? Vinnie and the music teacher knew each other?"

"Oh, that caused a ruckus. Vinnie was yelling at Bonnie and Bonnie's honey was yelling at Vinnie. It was crazy. I felt sorry for Bonnie's kid, watching all those grown-ass people making fools of themselves out in the front yard. Those kinds of shenanigans lower property values, you know."

Tabitha had nothing to say to that. Agnes pulled a blind down and peeked out the window. "Libby isn't finished yet?"

"Did she leave?"

"Yep. She's good at stealth-mode, huh?"

Tabitha ran to the window in time to see one skinny leg, then a spandex-encased bottom pop out of the neighboring window. Bonnie's window. *Oh no she did not.*

"There she is." Agnes banged on the window. "Come on. Hurry up."

Libby came in, still huffing from her exertions. "It's cold out there."

"So," Agnes asked, "What'd ya find out?"

"Not much. If they're gone they sure didn't take much. I mean, it looks like everything's there, but it's hard to tell. Those two were messy, like they were raised in a barn. Clothes everywhere, broken dishes—I don't know how people live like that. It's like the place was ransacked—"

The three women stared at each other open-mouthed as Libby's words sank in. Agnes sat down hard on the hot-pink sofa, the green muumuu poofing up around her middle.

"But look what I found." Libby rummaged around under her cape. "Voila!" With a flourish, she held out Tabitha's pink scarf. "Boy, I love that word." Tabitha flopped down beside

Agnes, mouth agape. "It is yours, right? I didn't pinch something that belonged to them, did I?" She dropped the scarf in Tabitha's lap.

Tabitha held it out. "Yes, it's mine. River had it. But how did it get in the trailer, unless River is involved?" She looked at Libby. "Are she and Skye friends?"

Libby shook her head. "Not that I know of. I never saw them together at school."

Agnes piped up. "That girl River would come out and they'd practice their flutes together. It was nice. And sometimes that music teacher would come out and help them."

What teacher goes to students' homes to rehearse? Why wouldn't they just practice at school? Tabitha buried her face in her scarf, overwhelmed. She pulled away, a curious expression crossing her face. She sniffed the scarf, then wrinkled her nose. Took another sniff. *That is definitely not my Chanel.*

"What are you doin'? Does it stink?"

"It smells like someone else's perfume."

Agnes grabbed the scarf and sniffed. "Ooh, that's the good stuff. It's that mango-vanilla that DeAnn sells."

"Who is DeAnn?" Tabitha rubbed her temples, her head pounding.

"You haven't been to DeAnn's Dress Depot? DeAnn owns it. She's fancy."

"I love her stuff. Let me smell." Libby tugged the scarf away from Agnes and sniffed. "She makes her own smells. Custom. And they're *ex-pen-sive.*"

"So not just anyone could buy this scent?"

"Oh no. Like I said—custom. She has these little samples for people to try, but once a smell is gone, it's gone. She puts it in lotions, candles, soaps..."

"I need time to sort all this out. Do you mind taking me home now?"

"Not at all." Libby hugged her sister. "I'll have the suit back ASAP. It worked real good. I might need to order one. Tabitha, you need one, too."

"I've never found much of a need for a catsuit."

"Well, you do now. You never know when we might need to go into stealth-mode again. Breaking and entering is pretty fun."

·········

Tabitha leaned her head against the Cadillac's headrest and closed her eyes. "Okay Libby, what do we know? Vinnie and Bonnie worked together and were friends. Vinnie knew Claire. Bonnie and Vinnie fought about her, and Agnes and Skye witnessed it. Vinnie and Claire are both dead. And somehow, in all this mess, River is involved."

"And Nick was sweet on Claire," Libby added. "But maybe Vinnie and Claire had something going on, so Bonnie killed them both and ran off."

"I've never met Claire, but I have seen Vinnie. Do you honestly think she and Vinnie might have had something going on?"

Libby shrugged. "No, I guess not."

"Besides, Gran had intimated Nick and Claire were a couple."

They rode in silence for the rest of the drive. Once at Gran's, Libby cut the headlights.

"Thank you for taking me out there."

"Sure, we should do it again. I had fun. I'm gonna have to order my own bodysuit, though. This one keeps creeping up my yaya, if you know what I mean."

Tabitha closed her eyes. *I'm afraid I do.*

Halfway out of the Cadillac Tabitha had a thought and ducked her head back in. "Hey, let's go to DeAnn's tomorrow. I'd like to find out who DeAnn sold that scent to."

"Sure," said Libby. "And we could have lunch at the cafe. Tomorrow is meatloaf and apple pie day. I'll pick you up at eleven-thirty so we can beat the rush."

·····•··•·····

The lights were off when Tabitha came in. She hung her coat and scarf on the old brass coat tree in the dark, then felt her way into the kitchen to make a cup of hot tea. She turned the light over the sink on, filled the kettle, then looked in Gran's cookie jar, hoping for a cookie, when she heard the front door softly open and close. *Nick must have been out also.*

She padded barefoot through the dining room as he was hanging up his jacket. "Nick?"

He jumped at the sound of her voice, knocking her scarf off the hook. "You scared me," he said, whisking it from the floor. He began to hang it back up but paused, holding it to his nose.

Is he sniffing my scarf?

Even in the dark, she felt his eyes boring into hers. He held her scarf out. "Do you have something to tell me?"

Tabitha blinked and opened her eyes wide. "No, nothing I can think of." She stretched and yawned. "Goodness—I didn't realize how tired I am. I better skip the tea. See you in the morning."

Chapter 17

The Plot Thickens

Tabitha couldn't fathom why Libby had the car windows down in the middle of winter. She wrapped her scarf around her neck, the scent of mango-vanilla wafting up. She wrinkled her nose.

"You don't like that smell?"

It's not Chanel, that's for sure. "It's great. Just more suitable for a young girl like River."

"I guarantee you River did not buy that."

Tabitha rested against the headrest. "Why do you say that?"

"For one, DeAnn's stuff is expensive, and two, DeAnn wouldn't sell to a teenager."

"So her mother bought it and River borrowed it."

"The thing is, DeAnn hates River's mother. DeAnn and River's mom, Amber, liked one of the Blackhorn boys in high school, but he ended up asking River's mom to the prom, and the ol' heifer's still salty. Says Amber stole him out from under her." Libby rolled her eyes. "Like anybody could trap a Blackhorn boy."

·····●·····

Several people glanced over as they entered the cafe. Today Libby wore royal blue snakeskin-patterned leggings, a tight orange sweater, and a blue feather boa with matching blue vinyl boots. "They can't keep their eyes off me. But I'm used to it," she said, by way of explanation as she waved to the room like a beauty queen.

Tabitha dug into her blue-plate special as soon as it was placed in front of her. The meatloaf practically melted in her mouth, just as Libby promised. *I'm going to end up as round as a basketball. Michael will be so smug.*

"What are you smiling about?" Libby patted her lips with the napkin, careful not to smear her tangerine lipstick.

"My ex. You know how some people unwind by watching TV or playing video games? I'm convinced he complained about my weight for entertainment, and if I keep eating like this, all his dire predictions will come true." Tabitha sipped her coffee.

"He doesn't know what he's talking about. You're adorable. So tiny, like Agnes. I'm cursed with this high-fashion model body. Sure, I got the fashion sense, but Agnes got all the looks."

Tabitha, coffee still in her mouth, made a loud snorting sound. *Please do not let me laugh.*

"You okay?"

Tabitha nodded, eyes directed at her saucer.

"Yeah, as cute as Agnes is, she has no style sense. Did you get a load of her get-up last night?"

Tabitha grabbed her glass of water and gulped it down.

"Girl," Libby scolded, "that's why you choke and snort. Slow down. You're drawing attention. It's embarrassing."

"Sorry. Are you going to get a piece of pie?"

"I'm thinking about it. How about we go over to DeAnn's first? I'm pretty full." Libby, waving the check above her head, hollered across the crowded cafe. "River, can you put this on my tab?"

··········

The ever-present bell tinkled as they opened the door to DeAnn's Dresses and Dungarees. A sweet, pungent odor immediately assaulted Tabitha's nose. *How could someone work here all day?*

A heavy-set woman greeted them, her hair bleached and teased into a yellow straw-like mess. Her eyes, ringed in heavy navy-blue eyeliner, gave her the distinct look of a pig. She'd applied foundation—two shades too dark—with a heavy hand, and topped everything off with a greasy and slightly smeared bright-pink lip gloss. Tabitha stifled the urge to hand her a tissue. *She looks like she's just finished a huge plate of fried chicken with her hands tied behind her back.*

"May I help you?" the woman said brightly. Her smile said welcome, but her eyes screamed *I'm judging you* as she looked over Libby's ensemble, then Tabitha's—both clearly lacking the fine fashion sense she possessed.

"Yes, Libby says you make custom scents."

"*Signature* scents."

"I'm interested. They sound amazing." Tabitha looked around but didn't see anything resembling a perfume counter.

DeAnn followed her gaze. "I keep them locked up. Let me get them." She disappeared behind a turquoise cow-print curtain. She shouted from the back room, "And you are…?"

"Tabitha Peterson," she yelled back.

DeAnn set a box of small glass vials on the glass counter. "Here are my newest," she gushed. "Each is my original proprietary concoction." She held one under Tabitha's nose. Tabitha sneezed. Repeatedly.

"Well." DeAnn managed to smile and look insulted all at once.

"I am so sorry. I must be allergic," said Tabitha, mortified.

"I am sure I use nothing that you could be allergic to." DeAnn sniffed, putting the testers back in the box.

"What about this one?" Libby reached across and plucked the vial labeled mango-vanilla from the box. DeAnn tried to grab it from her but Libby held it over her head. Tabitha thought for a minute that DeAnn might make a jump for it.

"That, I am afraid, is already claimed. It is no longer for sale."

Tabitha made a pouty face. "Mango-vanilla sounds lovely. Do you think it is the same fragrance as is on my scarf?"

"No, that's not possible."

Libby unscrewed the cap and held the vial out for Tabitha to sniff.

"Mmm... yummy. It smells like it to me." She held her scarf practically under DeAnn's nose. DeAnn jerked her head back but took the scarf. She closed her eyes and sniffed delicately.

"Where did you get this?" She eyed Tabitha suspiciously.

Tabitha balked, and Libby stepped in.

"It's her friend's scarf. Tabitha wanted to buy her more since she knows how much her friend loves it, and everyone knows how sensitive your nose is..."

"I see," she said, somewhat mollified. "A nice lotion? Bubble bath? A candle, perhaps?"

"Could you check and see what they already have?" Tabitha asked.

"Let me check my records." She pulled a notebook from a drawer and scanned a page, then stopped.

"Here we are. Body wash and perfume."

"Bubble bath would be nice," said Libby.

"Excellent choice. I will have it ready for pick-up by Wednesday if that works?"

"Would it be possible to have it delivered?" Tabitha asked, still working to find out who the scent belonged to.

DeAnn's eye twitched. "Of course. What is your address?"

Tabitha cut her eyes to Libby. *Help!* she mouthed.

"She will be out of town that day. Have it delivered directly to the recipient." Libby waved her hand in the air like she imagined a rich woman would.

DeAnn matched her beat for beat. Her fingernail hovered delicately over the page. Still looking down, she tapped the page several times before asking, "You are positive this is the fragrance?"

Tabitha cut her eyes toward Libby, nervous.

"Yes, " Libby answered.

DeAnn wrote out the receipt, noting the delivery address. "Spotted Wolf Dojo. I am sure Mr. Spotted Wolf will be delighted with your gift."

Tabitha caught Libby's gaze. *Great. We just ordered bubble bath for Nick.* She tapped her lip, as Libby blurted out, "Oh my gosh, I am so silly. You don't go out of town until next month. *Remember?*"

"Oh yes. Next month." Tabitha flapped her hands over DeAnn's head to get Libby's attention. *What?*

"So you can pick it up yourself, right?" Libby prompted.

"Yes! Yes. I will pick it up myself. Thank you so much, DeAnn."

....

The lunch crowd was gone, leaving the cafe almost empty. Tabitha and Libby sat near the window, their slices of apple pie largely untouched.

"Nick must have bought the fragrance for Claire." Tabitha tasted her coffee, then reached for two packets of sugar.

"Yeah, but that doesn't explain why your scarf smells like mango-vanilla." Libby took a bite of pie. "Or how it ended up in Skye's trailer. Maybe someone broke into Claire's house and stole her body wash."

"Who would break into someone's house to steal body wash?" Tabitha added milk and another packet of sugar to her coffee. It was not the best coffee she'd ever had.

Libby arched a brow. "Maybe they were after more than body wash, but just took it while they were there."

"Maybe. Atticus would have a record of any break-ins. Let's check."

A draft of cold air whooshed in as Coach Randall entered, wearing a camouflage jacket and orange ball cap. He ambled over to Libby and Tabitha's table.

"Hey, ladies. Fancy meeting you in a place like this. May I join you?" He unzipped his jacket and Tabitha jumped up before he could sit by her.

"No. We're leaving. Sorry. Come on, Libby. Gotta go."

"But it's on me. You can order anything you want. I've got big—pockets," he said, leering at both women.

"You wish," said Libby, flipping her hair. She pivoted and sashayed out, Tabitha close on her heels.

Once outside, Libby pointed a long, bony finger at Tabitha. "Girl, I've got your back, but he's kind of cute, and he offered to pay. I hear he's got tons of moolah. Why'd you do that?"

Tabitha tried not to think about Coach Randall and Libby together. She froze, her mouth shaped in a big O, and shook her finger at Libby. "His orange cap? Libby, he was the guy in Ryan's truck last night. Those two are up to something, I just know it. Let's step into the sheriff's office and see about that break-in."

"Atticus isn't there. I saw him leave while we were at the cafe."

"Even better. We can ask Yaeleen. You know, girl to girl."

"Yaeleen, how are you?" asked Tabitha, flashing a toothy smile. Yaeleen looked up from her paperwork, suspicious.

"I'm good. Can I help you?"

"Libby and I were at the cafe and thought we'd stop by to say hi."

"Hi." Yaeleen went back to work. Tabitha picked up the jar of jelly beans from her desk, but Yaeleen snatched it before Tabitha could unscrew the lid and slid it to the far side of her desk.

"Libby says this town is super safe, which got me wondering; what kind of crime do you deal with here? I'm sure this murder is unusual. Are there many break-ins?"

"Not too many." She kept typing.

"Have there been any recently?"

Yaeleen closed her laptop and leaned back in her chair. "I think it will be faster if you just ask me what you want to know, and then I can get back to work."

Tabitha could feel her cheeks getting warm. Libby elbowed her. Tabitha took a deep breath and plunged in. "Was Claire Reed's home burglarized?"

"Why would you ask that?"

"Just curious. Libby and I heard something over at the cafe and—"

Libby cut in. "Tabitha's scarf went missing and I found it. And now it smells like Claire's perfume, so we're wondering if someone broke in and stole it."

"From Gran's?"

"No, from Claire's place."

"Why would Tabitha's scarf be at Claire's? Have you two met?"

"No. We were just curious about the perfume." Tabitha glared at Libby.

Yaeleen leaned forward, placing her hands on her desk. "So you think we have a perfume thief in town?" Yaeleen looked from Libby to Tabitha, managing to look both annoyed and skeptical.

Tabitha reddened, feeling foolish. "Of course not. But maybe someone broke in looking for something else and took it. As a memento or something."

"Ms. Peterson, that's an interesting theory. I'm still not sure how your scarf could have gotten inside Claire's place. If memory serves me, you were hired because Claire went missing. No matter though; there was no report of a break-in." Tabitha studied Yaeleen's face, but it remained impassive. "Now may I get back to work?"

"Of course. Sorry to waste your time."

"We're here to serve."

Tabitha slid into Libby's Cadillac as Libby jutted her chin toward the truck parked next to her. "Ooh, look. That's Coach

Randall's Silverado. I wonder how he can afford that on a teacher's salary. That man's got to have money."

"Millie said he invested in the Happy Haze Pot Farm."

Libby concentrated on applying a fresh coat of tangerine lipstick before answering. "So I guess that's how he knows Ned Ryan."

"Maybe," Tabitha said without thinking, her focus inside the cafe. River was sitting in a corner booth across from Coach Randall, engaged in what looked to be a serious conversation. The girl dabbed at her eyes with a napkin. *Is she crying? This is getting weirder and weirder.*

Yaeleen looked out the door, watching the women drive away, then texted Atticus:

> Libby Lancaster and Tabitha Peterson were in, asking questions about Claire. I think we have a problem.

> On my way!

The Ranger pulled in, spraying gravel. "What happened?" Atticus demanded as he barreled through the front door.

"They wanted to know if there was a report of a break-in at Claire's."

He stood, one boot propped against the wall opposite Yaeleen's desk, arms crossed,
and rubbed his forehead. "What'd you tell them?"

"The truth. There was no report of a break-in."

"Why in the world would they ask that?"

"Well, here's the weird part. Peterson said her scarf went missing, and when she got it back, it smelled like Claire Reed's perfume."

"And how would she know what kind of perfume Claire wore?"

"That's a good question."

Atticus grabbed his hat. "Sounds like it's time to pay another visit to Ms. Peterson." He zipped his jacket up and pulled his cowboy hat low on his head. He opened the door to a burst of freezing wind. "Man, it's cold today."

"Yep. Hey, Atticus?"

"Yeah?"

"You gonna call this in?"

"No. At least not yet. You know, if the Feds would work with us even a little, we could have this thing wrapped up."

"Let me know if you find anything out."

"Will do."

Chapter 18

Confrontations

Atticus knocked on the front door, watching through the window panes as Gran shuffled through the dining room to open the door.

"Gran, you need to get some curtains. Your arthritis acting up?"

"It's not too bad. Come on in and get out of this cold. I'm making a pot of tea. Do you have time for a cup?"

"That'd be great." He followed Gran into the kitchen. Gran shuffled over to the cabinet and pulled down two china cups.

"But you aren't here for a cup of tea."

"No. I'm here to talk to Ms. Peterson if she's home."

"I believe she is. I'll make her a cup, too." Gran stood on her tiptoes to get the last cup in the back of the cabinet, but couldn't reach it. Atticus reached over her head and handed it to her.

"Thank you, Atticus. I'll go get her."

"Are you looking for me?" asked Tabitha, entering the kitchen.

"As a matter of fact, I am. Do you have a few minutes?" It wasn't a request.

Gran took the lid from the old brown cookie jar and arranged several sugar cookies on a plate. "I made them this morning. Why don't you two take your tea and cookies into the living room so you can have some privacy?"

"Thank you, Gran. I appreciate it." He held the door to the dining room open. "Tabitha?"

Atticus set the plate of cookies on the coffee table and got straight to the point. "Yaeleen said you and Libby came to the office with some questions about Claire Reed." Tabitha nodded, her mouth full of cookie. "I have a few of my own."

Tabitha swallowed hard. "Like what?"

"Why would you have an interest in Claire Reed at all?"

"Just curious, I guess."

"You told Yaeleen your scarf smelled like Claire's perfume. How would you know what kind of perfume she wore?"

"I don't. Libby said it smelled like something DeAnn's shop would carry, so we went in and asked.

"And DeAnn said she made it for Claire?"

Tabitha picked up her teacup, stalling while she thought. She'd never been a good liar.

"Not exactly." She sipped her tea, watching Atticus over the edge of her teacup. Atticus took a sip. Ate a cookie. Tabitha couldn't stand the suspense.

"Nick."

"Nick? What—he sniffed your scarf? Are you two seeing each other?"

Tabitha colored. "He knocked my scarf off the coat tree and noticed the perfume when he picked it up."

"And he said it was Claire's perfume."

"No, he did not."

"I don't like games, Ms. Peterson."

"I could see that Nick recognized the scent, and DeAnn said he'd purchased body wash and perfume, so I figured he bought them for Claire."

"And how did the scent make its way to your scarf?"

"I'm not sure." Tabitha tapped her mouth with her index finger, not sure what to say.

"Ms. Peterson, I'm waiting."

Tabitha took a big breath. "I forgot my scarf at the Sweet Shoppe and Skye picked it up. She seemed to like it so I let her have it. Then she doesn't show up for school, and River, the waitress at the cafe, walks into the band room wearing it. Then it turned up in Bonnie's trailer so I got it back, smelling like mango-vanilla. That's the whole story."

"I have the distinct impression there is a lot more to that story, but first I'd like to know how you got the scarf back."

"Libby brought it to me." She took a sip of tea, averting her eyes.

Atticus pushed. "Where did Libby get the scarf?"

"She didn't say." *Which is technically true. I think.*

"Tabitha, were you in that trailer? Let me remind you that trespassing is against the law."

"No."

"Then who got the scarf from the trailer?" Atticus's jaw twitched.

She tapped her lip and looked around. *I'm not going to throw Libby under the bus.* "I, uh—"

Nick's body filled the entryway from the foyer.

"Tabitha, you do not have to answer his questions. Atticus, it is time for you to go."

Tabitha could feel the hostility between the two men, and her own body tensed. Atticus nodded to Tabitha as he stood to leave. As he passed into the foyer he stopped, face to face with Nick, the animosity heavy.

Without taking his eyes off Nick's, he said, "Ms. Peterson, I am here to help you. I don't know what you're up to, but you need to stop. This is much more dangerous than you know. I will tell you this much: Claire Reed's body was found by the river, but that is not where she died. A very strong man moved the body after he murdered her."

"Get out," Nick growled. Atticus looked at Tabitha.

"Claire Reed died a slow, painful death. Whoever killed her, knew her, and didn't care if she suffered." Atticus reached for his hat and never saw it coming. Nick's punch, hard and lightning-fast, made a sickening crack as it connected with Atticus's jaw. Atticus stumbled but didn't fall. For a second, it looked like he would attack Nick, but instead, blood dripping from his mouth and nose, he turned to Tabitha once again. "I would lock my door tonight." He picked his hat off the floor and dusted it off. Gran, in the dining room, gripped a chair back, her face pale and taut.

"Sorry for the trouble, Gran." He pulled his hat low on his brow. "Ms. Peterson, we'll speak again."

That night Tabitha stared into the darkness, her brain bouncing from thought to thought every time she closed her eyes. *Nick found my glove down by the river that night. He had the time and no real alibi. Most of the town was at Millie's New Year's Eve party. Could he have..? No. I refuse to believe it. There is no way Nick could have killed Claire.*

She rolled onto her side and looked out the window. The sky was clear, the stars dazzling. *Why did I ever move here? What in the world was I trying to prove? I should be on tour with Zamarri, not worrying about a murderer.* Tabitha kicked off the blankets and sat by the window, looking out at the night. All that tea was having its effect. After she used the toilet, she quietly turned the lock on her side of the bathroom door. It never hurt to be careful.

She bolted upright, eyes wide open in the darkness.

River is the key. She had the scarf, which means she was in the trailer. She must have brought the music to the band room. Someone wants me to help. Skye? River? Who is 'A. Reed'? 'I'm Not Dead'. Is Claire alive? Of course not—what am I thinking-there's a body. Tabitha grabbed her laptop and typed in *Claire Reed*.

Well. I had no idea that Claire Reed is such a common name.

She typed in *Claire A. Reed*. Still too many hits. *Claire Reed obituary*. Nothing. *Claire Ann Reed. Claire Anne Reed.* Nothing. *Maybe Annette?* She glanced out the window. Pink streaked the sky, and she looked at the time. *Five o'clock. I need coffee.*

She padded down the stairs in her socks, careful not to wake anyone. She stopped halfway down. *Claire Annette Reed. That's too good. Wait until Zamarri hears this. She probably won't think it's funny. I've spent too much time with teenagers.* Tabitha took a sip of coffee. The door opened and Tabitha looked up, expecting Gran.

"I smelled coffee," Nick said, "and figured Gran was up. Sorry about the pajamas." He reached over her head to get a coffee cup, and Tabitha couldn't help but notice his chest and arms.

You are so buff. And smell so good. Tabitha could feel the heat between them and turned away, pulling her robe closed over her camisole. He stepped back at the same time, jostling her arm, and coffee sloshed over his tee shirt.

He jumped back and pulled his tee shirt off, drying his chest with a kitchen towel. "That is hot."

"Yes." Tabitha took a breath, and after a long second, looked away. "It is. It's hot." She could feel her cheeks burning. "The coffee. Coffee is hot."

Nick threw the towel in the sink and smiled. *He is so cute when he smiles.* He leaned against the sink and crossed his arms. Tabitha couldn't help but notice how thick and sinewy they were.

"Tabitha." Nick's demeanor changed. "I heard you moving around and wanted to talk to you before Gran woke up."

Tabitha frowned, curious. "Okay."

"I did not harm Claire. I... cared for her. Deeply. Be careful around Atticus." Their eyes met, each studying the other.

"I believe you. But why did you and Gran lie to Atticus the night he told us about her death? I know you went down to the river to look for my glove. And you lied to him about me. You don't think I had something to do with it?"

"No. Neither of us did, so why let him waste time on dead ends? I want the murderer found more than anyone."

Tabitha tapped her top lip, lost in thought, then said, "I have an odd question for you."

"Shoot."

"Did Claire ever tell you her middle name?"

"That is an odd question."

"But do you know it?"

"I do not. Why do you ask?"

Tabitha tapped her lip again, hesitant to tell him about the music, yet not sure why.

"You have a tell, you know," Nick said, a slight smile playing across his lips.

"A tell?"

"Yes. Every time you try to figure out what to tell someone, you tap your top lip."

"I do not."

"You do. Every time."

Tabitha brought her hand to her mouth, then froze.

"Oh my god. I do, don't I?"

Nick laughed. "Why do you ask about Claire's middle name?"

Tabitha decided to take the plunge and trust him.

"I've been getting messages. From an 'A. Reed'."

"When?" he asked, his eyes narrowing.

"This week at school. Someone left them on my piano."

"What did they say?"

"They're piano pieces. They were both titled, *I'm Not...* The notes for the first piece spelled out, *I'm Not... Bad,* and the second one spelled, *I'm Not... Dead..* Both were written by A. Reed."

"I don't get it."

"It's a message for a musician. For me."

"Do you still have them? Does anyone else know?"

"Just Millie and Libby."

Nick groaned. "If Libby knows, everyone knows."

"I don't think so. Libby is the one who figured it out. She can keep her mouth shut."

"Did you tell Atticus?"

Tabitha shook her head.

"And there's something else. I scoured the Internet but couldn't find anything about Claire's death. Could Claire have been her middle name?"

"I do not know."

"I think we need to figure out just who this A. Reed is."

Chapter 19

Closing In

It felt good to trust someone. Gran kept the coffee coming while Tabitha and Nick worked at the kitchen table all morning. Diagrams and sticky notes covered every space, with Tabitha and Nick yelling out when something new caught their attention.

"Are you two going to want lunch?" Gran asked.

"Is it lunchtime already?" Tabitha stretched her neck from side to side. Nick came around the table and stood behind her chair.

"Let me," he said, massaging her neck and shoulders.

It caught her off-guard but felt good. *This guy knows what he's doing.* "Gran, I hate to stop. Would you mind picking something up from the cafe?"

"Not at all. You two keep it up. You're going to figure this out." She grabbed her keys.

After the front door closed, Nick's hands felt too intimate and Tabitha jumped up. "Thanks. I feel much better," she said, leaning against the counter.

"You know, we need to set up a lesson time for you."

"Nick, I think it's great that you donated to the Winter Carnival, but I cannot stress this enough; I'm not a martial arts kind of girl."

"Do you think it's too violent?"

"No. Yes. No." Tabitha picked up a kitchen towel, folded it, and hung it back on the oven handle. "To be honest, I don't like to sweat. Ever."

One side of Nick's mouth went up a fraction. "Ever?"

Why do you have to be so cute? "Let me rephrase that. I do not exercise. It is not in my DNA. I come from a long line of non-exercisers."

"I do not believe you have never sweated."

"Not voluntarily. I don't like sports. I'm an artist. The only time I move is to have fun—like dance, with sweating an unfortunate side-effect."

"You're a dancer?"

"No. I've taken class, but I would never classify myself as a dancer."

"What kind of dance?"

'Ballet, mostly."

"Have you ever heard of a kata?"

Tabitha shook her head no.

"Come here."

"I don't think so," she said, wary.

Nick took her hand and led her to the center of the kitchen, then stood close behind her. She tried to turn her head to look at him but he moved his chest against her back and placed his hand against the side of her head.

"Look straight ahead. Relax." He took her hands in his, moving her arms in the air.

"What—"

"Shhh." He gently pushed her body forward with his, all the while moving her arms, nudging her this way and that as he went through the motions. As he led her through some sort of pattern, she let herself relax into it.

"Close your eyes and breathe," he whispered, continuing the movements.

At the end, he wrapped her arms around herself, encasing her entire body in his, then released her.

"What do you call that?" Tabitha asked, flushed and unable to make eye contact.

"Kata. Martial arts is not all kicking and sweating."

"It's beautiful. Do you promise I won't have to kick or sweat?"

Nick's eyes sparkled. "Not unless you want to," then, more seriously, "Come here. I will teach you one self-defense move today." He wrapped his arms around her and pulled her back against his chest so close she could feel his breath on her neck. "If you are ever in this predicament, grab his arm, stomp on the top of your assailant's foot as hard as you can, then immediately drop your weight and turn to face your attacker. Grab, stomp, and drop. I am going to walk you through it. Grab, stomp, and drop." Her first try felt awkward. "Yes, like that, but keep upright, do not bend your back. Aikido gives you everything you need. Remember that." He still held her against him. "We will not do anything you are uncomfortable with. Tae-kwon-do takes years to get proficient at, and the person with the longer reach usually wins, but Aikido is a small person's best friend in a fight."

Tabitha looked up, alarmed. "I am not fighting anyone."

Nick released her. "Good, because you would lose. But I can teach you how to get away if you ever get in a dubious predicament, or even better, how not to get in a bad situation to begin with. Think of it as 'No means No' with a bite."

Tabitha sighed. "Okay. But no sweating."

"Never."

Gran bumped the front door with her elbow, her arms full of sacks from the cafe. Nick immediately went to help. Halfway through the dining room, he said over his shoulder, "After lunch, we will go to the dojo and find you a gi."

A gi? What did I get myself into?

Nick opened the door and took the biggest bag.

"What are you smiling about?" Gran asked him.

"Do I have to have a reason to smile?"

"Usually." Gran smiled as she unpacked turkey club sandwiches, chips, and applesauce cake.

"So, have you figured anything out yet?" Gran asked between bites.

"It's a tangled web," said Tabitha. "Vinnie and Bonnie—Skye's mother—both worked at the Happy Haze, and both knew Claire Reed. Skye and River knew each other better than anyone imagined. Skye had my scarf, then River had it but lied about where she got it, and it ended up in Skye's trailer. Coach Randall is also connected to Happy Haze, at least as an investor, and Randall knows Ned Ryan, who also works there. And finally, I've been getting cryptic music messages from someone that goes by 'A. Reed'". But we still can't figure out why any of them would want to commit murder." Tabitha leaned on her hands, poring over the notes.

"Well, let's see," said Gran. "We could start with the easy questions. Tabitha, perhaps you could ask River at school. If she won't talk to you, then Nick, you can visit her mother. It might be less threatening since you're Native. Talk to her with her family. She's a good girl, and if she's involved, I'm sure she's in over her head and needs help. And Tabitha, could you get a look at Claire's personnel records to see if her middle name begins with an A? Maybe get her contact information?"

"That's confidential. I'll try, but I could get in big trouble if I'm caught."

"Then don't get caught," Gran said primly.

"Gran, I am shocked," said Nick.

"They aren't going to fire her. They need a music teacher. I'm being practical. I'll ask my sisters what they know about Happy Haze. That seems to be the common thread."

Nick looked at Gran admiringly. "Gran, you would have made a great detective. Right now I am going to run Tabitha over to the dojo and get her a gi. Do you need anything?"

"No thank you. I'm going to grab a book, make a nice cup of tea, and enjoy the rest of my Sunday. Have fun."

The dojo sat on a side street on the far corner of the town square in a converted Craftsman bungalow. The house, painted an unassuming gray with black trim, sat back from the street, and a small, neat sign proclaiming *Spotted Wolf Dojo* hung on the porch rail next to the steps. Tabitha hadn't noticed it before and said as much.

"We do not see what we do not look for," said Nick, opening the door. He turned the lights on. The floor was covered in gray mats, with mirrors mounted from one end of the room to the other. Tabitha didn't know what she expected something like a gym or locker room, but the dojo was neat and clean—and smell-free.

"Most kids leave their uniforms when they quit, so I keep them for students that cannot afford one. They are in here." They entered a large dressing room at the far end of the dojo. "I will leave you to find one in your size. Be sure it is roomy enough for kicking." Tabitha's eyes flashed and he laughed. "I know. No kicking."

The dojo exuded a serenity Tabitha hadn't expected, and she felt a little more comfortable with the idea of being alone in a room with Nick, and, besides, a gi was not exactly sexy. She looked in a mirror.

Ha, Michael, if you could see me now. I might even work up a sweat, just to spite you.

"Nick, does this one fit?" Tabitha padded over to his office in her bare feet. Nick looked up.

"The pants are the right length. Are they big enough for stretching and squatting?" Tabitha nodded. "Okay. Hold your arms out to your sides and turn your back to me."

Tabitha turned dutifully around. "Does it look okay?"

"Yes." She started to turn back around. "No, stay where you are."

"Why? Is it the wrong size?" She looked over her shoulder at him.

"No, it is the right size. You can change back now."

As Tabitha walked back to the dressing room, she caught her reflection in the mirror. The belt had loosened, and, with her arms down, the jacket gaped open, revealing more than a little skin and lace. Cheeks flaming, she put on her street clothes and folded the gi.

Nick was as stoic as ever as they left the dojo, and Tabitha avoided eye contact. Neither spoke on the drive back. Once on the porch, Nick spoke. "My early nights are Tuesdays, Wednesdays, and Thursdays. We can start this Tuesday. My last class ends at eight, so—eight-thirty?"

"That works."

At least Nick is gentlemanly enough not to mention the incident. She was halfway up the stairs before he called to her.

"Hey, Tabitha, on Tuesday—be sure to wear a tee shirt."

The door slammed shut and, for the first time in a long while, Nick Spotted Wolf laughed out loud.

Chapter 20
Sheep Pens

Nick dropped her off at school early. Tabitha sat in her office, the lights off, hoping the mystery person would leave another music clue. Her mind drifted to Nick. *This is ridiculous; I'm barely divorced.* The door to the band room opened quietly. A cell phone flashlight illuminated their way to the piano.

Tabitha flicked the light switch on just as a tall boy in a red flannel shirt and Wranglers laid the new piece down. He froze, wild-eyed.

"Good morning," said Tabitha. "Who are you?"

"I'm, uh... I'm... gone," he said, bolting from the room.

"Wait!" Tabitha ran to the door but the boy was nowhere to be seen.

A new title rested on top of the piano; *I Am...* by A. Reed. She read the music quickly. C-A-G-E-D-B-A-A-B-A-A. *I am caged baa baa.* Libby walked in waving a sheet of paper.

"I got her records. Ooh, is that a new clue? Let me see." She traded Claire's personnel records for the music. It only took her a few minutes to work it out. "Boy, this is a great clue," she said, handing Tabitha the music back.

Tabitha glanced at the top of Claire's personnel file, disappointed. "Her middle name is Lee. So we still don't know who 'A' is, and I don't get the *baa baa*."

Libby pulled the sheet music from her. "Are you serious? Now we know where she is." Tabitha looked at her, askance. 'A' is in the sheep pens." She waggled her eyebrows. "Let's go get her."

"What? Where are the sheep pens?"

"There's about six farms around here that raise sheep." Libby grinned broadly. "I guess we'll have to go check them out tonight. Stealth-mode?"

"Stealth-mode it is."

·····•·····

After dinner, Libby honked and Tabitha hopped into the Cadillac. Libby, dressed in basic black jeans and a turtleneck, still had her stocking cap and cape in the back seat.

"No bodysuit tonight?"

"I ordered my own. It comes in tomorrow." Libby shrugged delightedly. "I may have gotten you a little something, too. It's obvious you don't understand stealth-mode."

Tabitha looked down at her jeans and hoodie. "I am not wearing a catsuit. Besides, it's like thirty degrees out." Libby turned on a gravel road leading away from town. "Libby, shouldn't we wait until it's completely dark?"

"It will be by the time we get there."

"Where are we going?"

"I thought we'd hit a couple of little farms tonight. The Blackhorns account for most of the sheep around here, but I can't imagine anyone dumb enough to hide someone on their spread."

"Libby, did you figure out who the boy could be—the tall one wearing the flannel shirt and Wranglers?"

"Sure did. Turns out he's the son of the big guy that wears a ball cap." Libby cackled in the dark.

"Ha ha."

Libby turned off her headlights and pulled off the road, serious now.

"Tabitha, follow my lead. We do not want to get caught on someone's property at night."

"Got it. I don't want to end up in jail."

"Jail? People take care of things themselves around here. More likely we'll get shot. Now come on, and stay in the grass."

They gave the house a wide berth as they made their way behind the barn to an empty pen. A dog barked, startling them, and they hurried back to the car.

"Rats," Libby said, once back in the Cadillac. "We didn't think this through. No one is going to keep a person in an outside pen. Let's call it a night and start again tomorrow."

"It's still early. Let's at least try one more."

Libby eased the Cadillac back toward town. "There's just two places big enough to have indoor sheep pens. One is the Randall place."

"Coach Randall?"

"Yeah. He bought it up when he came into his pot money."

"Who has the other one?"

"The Blackhorns. And the Blackhorns have security."

"There's no way the sheriff would keep someone hostage. I say we check out Coach Randall's."

"Did you bring a gun?"

"Of *course* I did not bring a gun."

"Me neither. Agnes is the dead shot in the family. Maybe I can talk her into coming with us tomorrow night."

"Absolutely not. There will be no weapons." Tabitha leaned her head against the headrest, eyes closed. "Trespassing, guns... This is too much. Let's go to Atticus tomorrow. We don't have any business doing this stuff. We're teachers. We'll lose our jobs if we get caught. We need to let the authorities handle this."

Libby swerved onto the side of the road, hitting the brakes so hard Tabitha hit her head against the side window. "Ow," she said, holding her head.

"Now you listen to me. There is someone out there in a cage, and it could be Skye. But whoever it is, they are depending on us to find them. And there is a good chance they are on Blackhorn property, so we cannot go to Atticus. Two people are dead, and whoever is in that cage may be the third. Do you want that on your hands?"

"No." Tabitha tenderly touched the lump already forming on her forehead.

"Okay then. Tomorrow I'll pick you up and we'll go to the Randall place."

Tabitha nodded reluctantly. "Okay, but do you think we can be back before eight-thirty? I've got an, um, thing. And wait for me behind the laundromat. I don't want anyone to know I'm gone."

"Sure." Libby pulled up in Gran's drive and placed her hand on Tabitha's arm. "We're going to find Skye. We may be just a couple of teachers, but we're smart ones. And we're certainly smarter than Coach Randall."

Nick opened the door for her. "Were you able to get Claire's records?"

"Libby did. They're upstairs." She pulled off her hat and hung her coat on the coat tree.

"Whoa, where did you get that goose egg?"

Tabitha touched it gingerly. "Ow. Libby's driving?"

"That has got to hurt. I will get something for it while you get the records."

Tabitha, head throbbing, leaned back on the sofa. Nick came back with a bag of peas wrapped in a kitchen towel, ibuprofen, and water. He handed her the glass and pills, then picked up Claire's records from the coffee table.

"Hmm. Everything looks ordinary."

She opened one eye. "I know," she said, trying not to move her head.

"So.... nothing."

"I think it's something. We have her middle name, her former address, and emergency contact info. That's more than we did have."

"I hate to ask you right now, but did you have a chance to talk to River?"

"She wasn't at school," said Tabitha, her eyes shut. "I'll talk to her tomorrow, for sure. I'm sorry, but I've got to go to bed." She stood, instantly sorry she had. "Ow. Ow. Ow." She closed her eyes once again, dizzy.

"Are you okay?"

"I'm fine; I just stood up too fast. Low blood pressure— the small person's curse."

"You do not look fine. Maybe you should stay home tomorrow."

"I'll be okay by morning. I'm just exhausted."

"You have a head injury. You should not go to sleep. How about we watch a movie."

"Gran doesn't have a television set."

"There is one in my room. Stay awake at least as long as the movie, then you can go straight to bed. Come on, I am helping you up the stairs."

Tabitha began to protest but thought better of it. "Deal."

············

The aroma of freshly baked sweet rolls greeted Tabitha as she came downstairs the next morning.

Gran stopped pouring coffee when she saw Tabitha's face. "Oh dear, what happened to you?"

"Libby's driving. Does it look that bad?"

Nick looked up from the paper. "Yes."

"It's purple. Honey, are you sure work is a good idea?" Gran handed her a coffee cup.

"I am." She sat down gingerly. "I would like some ibuprofen if it's no trouble."

Nick said, "If you change your mind and need to come home, give me a call. I am going to stick around here and do a little research on Claire."

Tabitha nodded, then wished she hadn't. "Once I get to work, I'll forget all about it."

"Sure you will."

Tabitha barely made it to the band room before the bell rang. Band kids were already warming up. *Oh good. The dulcet sounds of high school band. Just what I need.* Tabitha watched River pull her piccolo case from under her chair and almost panicked. *No, no, no. I cannot do this today.*

"Okay, band. We're not playing." The moaning began. "It's air band day. Practice on your own silently, because we're having a chair test tomorrow. River, I'm glad you're back. May I see you in my office?"

"Ms. Peterson, what happened to your head? Are you okay?" River asked, her face all concern.

"It's nothing. I just didn't think I could handle brass and percussion today. Especially the saxophones." River laughed, waiting for Tabitha to go on. "River, have you ever auditioned for All-State?"

"Yes, this will be my third year."

"And have you ever entered the Solo & Ensemble contest?" River nodded and Tabitha continued. Do you already have a piece for this year?"

"Skye and I were working on a duet, but now..." River shifted from one foot to another.

"Have you heard from Skye?"

"Mmm..." River's gaze darted to the door as if she wanted a fast escape.

"I've been concerned about her. Is she sick?"

River shrugged noncommittally.

"I went out to her trailer. It looked deserted, but her mother hasn't contacted the school."

"Hmm." River looked around the room like she'd never seen it before. "Can I go practice now?"

"River, I think you know where she is, and I think she needs help." River's eyes filled. "She could need help, and I suspect you might, too. Do you want to shut the door and tell me?"

River carefully closed the door. Tabitha motioned to a folding chair. "Have a seat."

The girl's face crumpled. "Ms. Peterson, we're in real trouble."

Chapter 21

Catsuits

It took Tabitha longer than she'd thought it would to tidy her desk, and the parking lot was almost empty as she left the building. Libby already in her car, waved. Tabitha waved back, then spotted Nick's truck idling and pointed to it, mouthing *one minute*. He rolled down his window.

"I am on my way to talk with River's mother and older brother. It turns out they both work at the Happy Haze." He noticed her shivering, and asked, "Why aren't you wearing a coat?"

"I didn't need one this morning."

"It's January."

"Still didn't need one. When I left it was sixty degrees."

"Well, it is now thirty-eight. Get in. I can swing by the house and drop you off first," he offered.

"You go on ahead. I'm going to have dinner at Libby's."

"Will you be up for your lesson?"

"I wouldn't miss it. Eight-thirty, right?"

Nick gave her a thumbs-up and pulled away.

Libby unlocked her Cadillac. "Come on. Hurry up."

As soon as Tabitha shut the car door, Libby reached into the back seat and grabbed an Amazon box. "They came in last night. We can swing by my place and put them on."

Tabitha looked at the box, wary. "What is this?" She wasn't sure she wanted to know the answer.

"Catsuits. We're going full stealth-mode tonight. Are those your shoes?"

"Of course they're my shoes. I'm wearing them. Why?"

"I just think heels will be hard to sneak around in. Especially on a farm. But, boy, you'll look sexy."

"I'm not changing clothes."

Libby pulled to the back of a large house and parked in front of a two-story garage apartment. "Here's my place. It's not much, but it's home, as they say. I thought we could make sandwiches. I even bought pickles." Libby unlocked the door and tossed her satchel on the sofa, then tore into the package. She pulled out two black lycra body suits in plastic bags, squinting to see the sizes. "This one's yours." She threw it to Tabitha, who threw it straight back.

"Libby, I am not putting on this ridiculous outfit. I'd feel like an idiot."

Libby looked as if Tabitha had struck her in the face. "But I wore Agnes's the other day. I didn't know you thought I looked like an idiot." She swiped at her eyes. "I'll send them back."

"Oh, give it to me," Tabitha snatched it from her. "It won't hurt to try it on."

Libby beamed. "Nope, not one bit." She pulled her top off.

"Um, I think I'll change in the bathroom."

"Sure. You go right ahead." She stripped off her pants and wiggled into her suit before Tabitha could even close the bathroom door. "I'll make the sandwiches. Come out once you get it on."

A few minutes later Libby hollered, "Do you like tuna?"

"Tuna is fine," said Tabitha as she entered the kitchen.

"Woo-hoo, you look fancy. Have you seen yourself? You should wear catsuits all the time."

"Libby, this is an actual *cat* suit." She turned in a slow circle. "I have a tail. You do not have a tail. Why do I have a tail, Libby?"

"Well, you *said* catsuit. Personally, I think it's a little over the top, but you do you, girl." Libby took great pride in adopting whatever slang the high school kids were saying. She held up the paper bag with the sandwiches. "Let's go."

"I'm not— I can't— I won't—"

"Won't what? Where's your coat?"

"I didn't need one this morning."

Libby disappeared into her bedroom. Tabitha could hear drawers opening and closing.

Libby came back waving something black. "Here." She threw a sweater at her. "Put this on and let's go. It's getting dark."

Tabitha sighed. The sweater hung to her knees. *Oh well. I'll look like I'm wearing a dress and leggings. I'll just wrap my tail around my waist.*

"Surprise!" Libby threw her a package. Tabitha tore it open to find a black knitted hat and mittens.

"Oh, good. Thank you. I thought the cold front wasn't hitting until tomorrow." She pulled the hat out of the package and held it up. "It has ears."

"I know. And look at the mittens. They're little paws." Tabitha pulled the hat on, two ribbons dangling. Libby tied them in a bow under Tabitha's chin. "There," she said, delightedly. "I looked all over for that. They didn't come in adult sizes or I would have gotten a set for myself, too."

Great. I am wearing a child's kitty hat and paw mittens. With my tail. I am about to commit a crime wearing the exact same Halloween costume I wore when I was five.

Libby opened the front door. "We better get a move-on." Tabitha looked around to make sure no one saw her, then darted into the car.

"That's the spirit!" Libby chortled. "Stealth-mode all the way!"

·····●·●·····

The wind blew from the north and as ridiculous as she knew she looked, the hat and mittens kept her toasty. Libby pulled to the side of the road when they got to Coach Randall's. An old barbed-wire fence ran completely around the farm.

"Hold the top wire up and I'll climb through," said Libby. Tabitha held it as high as she could, careful not to poke herself. Once through, Libby stepped on the bottom wire for Tabitha. "Come on."

Tabitha had one leg and arm through when they heard a truck coming down the road.

"Hurry," Libby whispered. Headlights shone over the hill. "Duck, duck," Libby ordered urgently, pressing her face against Tabitha's back. The truck drove past and Libby breathed out. "Whew. They didn't see us. Come on."

"I can't."

"What?"

"I'm hung in the barbed wire."

"Oh dear. I must have dropped the wire when I ducked." Libby got out her phone. "The barbs are all tangled up in your sweater."

"Well, untangle them." *Why did I agree to this?*

Libby pulled on the wire.

"Ow. Be careful. They're scratching my back."

"Ouch. I just stuck myself. These barbs are sharp. It might be a good idea to get tetanus shots tomorrow."

"*Just untangle them,*" Tabitha repeated through gritted teeth.

"I don't think I can. You should probably just shuck the sweater. Can you wiggle out of it? Here, I'll hold the arms. There ya go. Good job."

Tabitha stood inside the fence, glowering. "Let's get this over with. I'm freezing. Wait; the barn door faces the house. How are we going to get in without being seen?"

Libby waggled her eyebrows mysteriously. "I have my ways. Just follow me." Clearly, Libby was enjoying herself. They sneaked around the far side of the barn, avoiding the house the best they could. "Here. We'll go in through the pen in the back. See that door?"

Tabitha looked around the pen. "Do you mean the gate to the pen?"

"No. Inside the pen. The little door at the bottom of the barn."

"That is a cat door. For cats." She could see Libby grinning. Gleefully. "Do not say it."

Libby snickered. "You're little. Just climb into the pen and scoot through."

"Libby—"

"Just go."

Tabitha scampered over the fence, surprised she found it so easy. She did not expect the mud on the other side. She slipped and landed on her stomach. She picked herself up, covered in muck.

"I told you those heels weren't stealthy. I mean, they're cute and all, but not practical."

"Libby?"

"Yes?"

"Shut up."

Inside the barn, Tabitha realized she didn't have her phone. "Hey," she whispered into the darkness. "Is anybody here? Skye? Miss Reed?" Nothing. She felt her way along the wall until she found a light switch, but didn't dare turn it on. *I'll just turn it on super quick. In case they're drugged, or asleep.* She turned the switch on and bright light flooded the barn. Empty. No person, no cage—not even a sheep or pig. Disappointed, Tabitha switched off the light. Temporarily blinded, she felt her way back along the opposite wall and accidentally kicked a metal can. Dogs started barking. Tabitha froze, listening. A screen door opened and the dogs burst out, barking furiously at the barn door.

"What is it? Who's in there?" The barn door scraped open and the dogs rushed in as Coach Randall, rifle in hand, flicked the light on. He frowned, scratched his belly where his tee shirt didn't reach his pajama pants, and burst out laughing. The dogs had her cornered, her face pale—where it could be seen through the mud.

"Rufus, George—it's okay." He patted his thigh and the dogs came running.

"Now look what we have here, boys. What are you doing in my barn, little kitty?"

Chapter 22
The Price To Pay

A good offense is the best defense. She had learned that much from Michael. "I know you have a hostage," she blurted out.

"What? A hostage? Who am I keeping hostage?"

"I'm... I'm ah... you know who it is." Tabitha's stomach flip-flopped as she realized she didn't know who she was looking for.

"That's a serious allegation coming from a lady in a kitty costume," he said, amused.

"And I know you're involved with the pot farm," she said, hoping she sounded confident.

"So?"

"And the murders of Vinnie and Claire Reed."

Randall quit laughing and pulled out his phone.

"What are you doing?"

"First, I'm taking a picture of you, then I am calling the sheriff. You're trespassing on my land."

"Oh no. Don't do that. Please don't do that."

"Hey, Atticus," he said into the phone, "It's Randall. I have an intruder. A cat burglar, you might say. I'm sending a picture. You're gonna want to see this."

Tabitha closed her eyes and leaned her head against the barn wall, deflated. *This could not possibly get any worse.* She opened them just in time to see Libby sneak up behind Randall and clock him on the head with a shovel. *I misspoke. It can definitely get worse.* Rattled, Coach Randall stumbled, then shook his head and turned to grab the weapon from his assailant, only to find Libby staring at him in disbelief.

"Huh. I thought for sure that would knock you clean out."

Coach looked at Tabitha, then back to Libby and raised his rifle. "What the hell? Get over there by Ms. Peterson, where I can keep an eye on you both." He rubbed his head, glancing around suspiciously. "Is there anyone else?"

"No, it's just us," said Tabitha as she slid down the wall.

Libby squatted beside her. "You kicked the bucket."

Tabitha rolled her eyes.

"Don't talk." Tabitha put her head in her hands, waiting to be arrested.

They heard a vehicle on the gravel drive, then a door slammed, and Atticus came around the side of the house.

"Your burglar in there?"

"Yes. Both of them."

"Put your weapon down. I'll take it from here. " Atticus stopped cold when he saw who the burglars were He holstered his firearm and rubbed a hand across his face. He looked at Randall, speechless.

Coach threw out his arms. "I know. Not what I expected, either."

"How—? Why—?" Atticus's brow furrowed. He rubbed his face again.

Everyone started talking at once. Atticus pointed at the two women. "Both of you, hush. Coach?"

'My dogs started raising a ruckus so I got my rifle and came out here to find Ms. Peterson dressed like this. Then Miss Libby sneaked up behind me and hit me over the head with a shovel. And here we are."

"Miss Libby, why in the world would you hit Randall with a shovel?"

"Well, I thought it would knock him out."

"Why—? No." Atticus scrunched up his face before proceeding. "Ms. Peterson, would you like to explain?"

"It's... complicated?"

Atticus turned to Coach Randall. "Do you have any idea...?"

"None. Maybe a role-playing game? I've heard about them from the students."

Atticus took a deep breath, held it, then exhaled noisily. "You ladies know trespassing is a crime. As is hitting people with shovels. Coach, you want to press charges?"

Randall cocked his head and looked at Tabitha for a long minute before he shook his head. "No, I don't believe I do."

Libby blew out air. "Well, I guess we'll be going, then. Have a good night." She lifted her head defiantly as she passed, Tabitha trailing in her wake.

Atticus raised his eyebrows as he noticed her tail for the first time. "Miss Libby, you can go on, but I'm taking Ms. Peterson home."

"I need to go with Libby. My clothes are at her house." The last thing Tabitha wanted was to go with Atticus.

He scanned her from ears to tail. "I don't care. It's just lucky I came in Yaeleen's squad car; you're a muddy mess."

"You can't expect me to go home like this."

"You can thank Coach Randall that you aren't going to jail." He opened the back door. "Get in. And watch your tail."

·········

Atticus didn't speak the entire drive back. They pulled up to the house, the squad car's lights still flashing. Nick appeared on the porch, Gran right behind.

"What is going on?" he demanded the minute Atticus got out of the car.

Atticus said nothing, just opened the back door and pulled out a bedraggled Tabitha. She stood in the yard covered in muck, her kitty hat skewed to one side, her tail hanging, wringing her paw mittens.

"Take her. She better be in my office first thing tomorrow morning." He shook his head, slammed his car door, and drove away.

"It's a funny story—" Tabitha began.

Nick cut her off. "It is not. You did not show up for your lesson." She looked up, shocked at the sharpness in his voice. His eyes were dark and stormy. "Gran, I am going to take a drive."

"Be safe. Tabitha, go clean up. I'll make tea." said Gran, her words clipped.

"Is he that mad because I missed a lesson?" Tabitha asked after the door slammed.

"He's not mad. Go take a shower."

"He looked mad to me," she persisted.

"Are you that dense?" Gran's eyes flashed. Tabitha stepped back as if she'd been slapped. She'd never seen this side of Gran. "You didn't show up when you know a murderer is running loose, and then Atticus pulls up in the squad car with his lights flashing? Nick just lost Claire. You don't think things through. Go clean up." Gran turned on her heel and went into the kitchen.

Gran's words haunted her as she showered, her tears mixing with the hot water. *That is exactly what Michael always says; I don't think things through. It's true. I don't have any business in Medicine Creek. What am I doing here? I've never lived in a small town in my life. I'm a classical musician. A musician that threw away a chance to go pro. Why didn't I practice? Why didn't I audition? That's what I'm meant to do, not be someone's wife or teach kids who don't want to learn. Or get myself involved with murders and missing teenagers.. Zamarri is right; I sabotage myself. I'm going to practice every day, finish out the school year, and then move back to the city. I could live with my mother again while I audition. I have talent. Skye is right, too—my talent is wasted here.*

⋯⋯⋯⋯⋯

A pot of tea sat on the little white table by her bed. *Even when Gran's mad, she's kind.* Tabitha wrapped herself in her quilt and picked up her phone, then set it back down. *I am not going to call anyone and whine. This is all my own doing. I'll get out of it by myself.* She heard the outside door on Nick's side quietly open and close. *Now I've ruined our friendship. What a mess I've made.* Tabitha laid her head down, inhaling the fresh cotton smell of her sheets, and cried herself to sleep.

Her screams woke him. Nick ran into her room ready to fight, but it must have been a bad dream. "Tabitha, wake up. *Tabitha.*"

She opened her eyes, uncomprehending. The light from the bathroom obscured his face; all she could see was the outline of a man looming over her. She opened her mouth to scream again.

"Tabitha, it is me. It is okay." She looked tiny in the bed. Tiny and helpless, like a scared little animal. Without thinking, he sat on the bed and scooped her up into his arms. He could feel her shaking as he rocked her. "It is okay. You are safe. I have you. It is okay." He stroked her hair, his own loose and silky against her face and shoulders. She sniffed.

"You use my shampoo."

Nick laughed, releasing her. "But not your soap." He pushed her hair from her face. "Are you better now?"

She shook her head yes.

"Do you want to talk about it?"

"Not now. Maybe in the morning."

"Lay down. Everything will be fine. Do you want me to leave the bathroom doors open?"

"That'd be nice."

He stood, his back to her, and stretched, his hair dipping to his waist. She watched as he left her room.

She lay in bed, miserable and unable to go back to sleep. After a time she padded into his room.

"Nick," she whispered, standing next to his bed. "Nick, are you awake?"

"Mmm?" He moaned, groggy.

"Can I sleep in here?"

He pulled the blankets aside enough for her to scoot in. She nestled against him, her body soft and warm, and immediately fell fast asleep. Nick, however, looked at the ceiling the rest of the night, fully aware that a beautiful woman lay beside him.

Chapter 23
Day Off

Nick, already on his second cup of coffee by the time she made it downstairs, asked, "Breakfast?"

"No, I'm late. I didn't hear my alarm. I need coffee. Can you still take me? I should call and tell them I'm on my way. I can not believe I slept in."

Nick set his cup down. "I already called them."

"You did? When?"

"When I turned off your alarm. Biscuit?"

"Why did you do that?" She took a biscuit and Gran passed her the butter.

"You had a rough night. I could hear you getting up and down a lot. I am right next door, you know." He winked at her.

Nick winked at me?

"You need a day off. Gran and I decided we are taking you to see the horses. It is beautiful out, so eat your breakfast, then go change out of your work clothes."

No one is saying anything about last night. Be grateful for little things.

Gran said, "Take your time. I've got an errand to run. Let's plan on one o'clock?"

"That's perfect. I decided it's time I start practicing again—if it won't bother anyone?"

"Anytime. We both love music. Now I need to get a move on." Gran kissed Nick on the cheek. "Back in a flash."

··········

It must have been eighty degrees inside Gran's Buick and Nick had the windows rolled down. His braid hung over the back of his seat, and Tabitha, riding in the back, touched it, thinking of how he looked last night with his hair loose. Gran caught her eye and she jerked her hand away.

"Sweetie, in our culture it's disrespectful to touch someone's braid without asking."

"I am so sorry," Tabitha said, blood rushing into her cheeks. She glanced into the rearview mirror, horrified to find Nick watching her, a twinkle in his eye.

The countryside was beautiful. Cows dotted the fields, enjoying the early afternoon sun, and birds drifted lazily above the fields.

"We froze to death yesterday, and today it's seventy degrees," Tabitha said, trying to change the subject.

"Welcome to Oklahoma," Gran quipped.

"Where are we going?"

"Out to Lenore's. She has land. She started a horse rescue a long time ago, then branched out to include mustangs."

"There's still wild horses?"

"Oh yes," said Gran. "She takes after our father."

Tabitha leaned forward from the back seat. "Did he raise horses?"

"He did, but I meant Lenore lives close to his ways. We're Comanche."

"I wondered if you were Native, but you make such great Mexican food." Tabitha clapped her hand over her mouth. "Oh my god, that came out wrong."

"It's okay. My mother came from Juarez. She taught me to cook."

"So Nick, you're Comanche?"

"I am Chickasaw and Cherokee."

"So you two aren't related?"

Gran glanced at Nick, who kept his eyes on the road.

"I'm sorry. I shouldn't have asked." Tabitha sat back. "It's none of my business. I don't want to ruin the day."

Nick answered. "Gran took me in when I was a boy." He didn't elaborate and Tabitha let it drop.

·············

Lenore and Estelle were in the kitchen when they came in. Nick sniffed the air.

"Do I smell fry bread?"

"You might. Come on back," Estelle shouted. Nick laughed and hugged her. "Thank you, Auntie. You make the best fry bread." Tabitha had never seen Nick so relaxed and happy.

"What about me? I am the eldest elder." Nick released Estelle and threw his arms around Lenore.

"No disrespect intended, Auntie," he said, showering her with kisses.

"None taken, but you still get to muck out the stalls after lunch," she laughed and pushed him away. "Now go away while I work."

Tabitha and Gran cleaned up after lunch so Estelle and Lenore could sit in the living room and put their feet up, while Nick tended to a few chores outside.

"I love your family," said Tabitha, rinsing the last glass. "You're all so loving and..." she searched for the word, "*happy.*

It's sure not like any of my family gatherings." She handed the glass to Gran.

"Tabitha, our people have lost a lot. Our family has lost a lot. But we refuse to let anyone take our joy. We cherish our time together, our memories. There is so much sadness in the world. I can tell you've had your share of pain, but remember, no one can take your joy. If you aren't careful, you can lose it, but if you cherish it and treat it like the gift it is, it is yours forever. But I think using it is the secret. You can't keep it locked away, waiting for special occasions. Using it makes it grow stronger, and it multiplies."

Nick came in through the mud room, stomping his feet. "You two finished up? Who all is going to see the mustangs?"

Lenore's voice echoed through the farmhouse. "Wild horses couldn't keep me away!"

Estelle hollered back, "Are you ever going to get tired of that joke?"

Lenore, decked out in jeans and flannel, was in the mud room, putting on her boots. She caught Gran's attention through the open doorway, and both shouted back, "*Never!*" It was a good day.

··········

Nick drove them home as Gran dozed in the back seat.

"Thank you. I needed this more than I knew. Your family is wonderful."

"I am fortunate." A trace of a smile played across his face as he glanced at Gran from his rear-view mirror. "They live close to the land. It has been in the family for generations, but it is a struggle to hold on to it."

Tabitha looked at him curiously but said nothing.

Nick explained. "There is oil on it, and our good state is always on the side of the big oil companies."

They drove in companionable silence as the sun sank over the town.

"I think Oklahoma skies are the prettiest I've ever seen."

"I agree, but it is my home." As they neared the town, Nick asked, "What happened last night?"

"Skye hasn't been at school and I thought Coach Randall kidnapped her. Or someone. Maybe A. Reed, whoever that is. So I went out to investigate."

"Why Coach Randall?"

"I got a new piece of music yesterday. It said, *I'm Caged Baa Baa*. Libby figured it meant sheep pens, and she said the only farms big enough to have inside pens were Randall's place and the Blackhorn place, and I figured it couldn't be Atticus."

"Why did you keep it from me?"

"I didn't mean to. You were taking River home and Libby and I just got caught up in the moment. What did you find out at River's?"

"I talked to her mother, Amber. She and her son both work at the pot farm, and they believe there is something illegal going on out there."

Tabitha interrupted. "Did you find out what?"

"Yes. It is not a pot farm. They are growing hops and passing it off as pot."

"Why?"

"It is legal to sell hops across state lines. It is not legal to sell marijuana across state lines."

"But that's still fraud."

"Yes, but who is going to call the Feds and tell them they were duped while trying to buy commercial quantities of marijuana illegally?"

"Good point."

He continued. "River's mother and brother were discussing it one night and things got a little heated. River woke up and overheard."

"What they were arguing about?"

"Tabitha, they are good people and do not like what is happening out there. River's brother wanted to tell the authorities, but Amber was afraid they would lose their jobs. This is a small community and work is scarce, especially jobs with benefits. River told Skye, and they called the FBI with an anonymous tip last summer, but the FBI did not take action. And once people started dying and disappearing, no one was willing to talk. River told her mother everything last night and they are both frightened to death."

"And now Skye and Bonnie are missing."

"Not exactly. Skye's mother took off but Skye wouldn't leave River. She is hiding somewhere and River knows where she is, but will not tell. It is her way of keeping her safe."

"Wow. That's a lot for two young girls to shoulder."

They drove for a while in the darkness, each contemplating the recent events, before Nick smiled in the dark. "May I ask why you were wearing a cat costume?"

"Libby got it for me. Calls it stealth-mode."

Nick held up his hand. "You make a very cute cat."

"That was the most embarrassing experience of my entire life."

"I am confused as to why you would take Libby with you. She is a bit—elderly."

"I may not have thought things through," she said wryly. "But I'm glad she was there. There's no telling how things might have gone if she hadn't hit Coach Randall with the shovel."

"What? Why would she do that?"

"She thought he was going to shoot me."

He pulled into the drive and cut the engine but did not get out. "Randall pulled a weapon on you?" he asked, looking straight ahead. "That explains the nightmare."

Not really. I dreamed Michael and Zamarri came to Medicine Creek and Michael put me in a cage, and Zamarri wouldn't stop laughing. And my mother just stood there—smiling the whole time—telling everyone it was fine because I was safe.

"In his defense, Randall thought there were burglars in his barn." She could feel the day's camaraderie dissipating and her shoulders slumped. "Look, it was a stupid thing to do. I know I don't think things through, and I'm never going to do anything like that again. I already decided I'll finish out the year—because I am determined to finish at least one thing I start—but then I'm going to move back to my mother's and audition until I find a position." Nick opened his door without commenting. She reached over and touched his arm. "You aren't mad, are you?"

He covered her hand with his. "No, Tabitha, I am not mad." He opened the door to the back seat and patted Gran's shoulder. The older woman looked around, confused, and he smiled at her. It was the saddest smile Tabitha had ever seen.

Chapter 24

Busted

The school secretary tapped on the band room door. "Tabitha, you're needed in the office."

"Now? Second grade is on their way." Tabitha frowned.

"Yes, now. I'm here to watch your class."

Tabitha saw Atticus's cowboy hat in the principal's office and took a breath. *This is not good.*

"Come in," Roundtree called through the open door. He did not sound happy.

A hot-pink lizard print leg with a red high-heel attached swung back and forth. *That does not bode well.*

"Sit," Roundtree said, pointing to the empty chair. Atticus tipped his hat before putting it in his lap. Roundtree stared at Tabitha's now yellow-green lump. "I understand there has been an incident." Tabitha looked at Libby, who sat, wide-eyed, as if she had never heard of any such thing. "Sheriff Blackhorn here asked you to talk to him yesterday, which neither of you did, so he is here to escort you to his office. But before you leave, I want you both to know I've already talked with the school board, and we feel it best that you are both suspended until this is resolved, at which time we will consider our avenues. You have brought shame to this school."

Libby held her hand up. "Wait right there. What about Coach Randall? Why isn't he in here?"

Roundtree sniffed. "As I understand it, Coach Randall was the victim, Miss Lancaster. He felt it his duty to call the school board members yesterday. Now, will you please excuse me?"

"Are you ladies ready?" Atticus mock bowed.

"Now I wish I'd hit Coach Randall harder," Libby said loudly.

"Libby," Tabitha whispered, "Quit talking."

··•••••··

Libby sat with Yaeleen while Atticus interviewed Tabitha in his office. She told him everything she knew.

"I still do not understand why you got involved in this in the first place. You aren't even from this town," said Atticus.

"I was concerned about Skye. Everything just snowballed after that."

"Do you still have the music messages?"

Tabitha nodded. "They're on the piano at school."

"And you don't know who sent them?"

"No. A boy I've never seen before brought the last one. May I ask you a question?"

"Sure. I may not answer it."

"Why do you think Randall called the school board members but didn't press charges? That doesn't make sense."

Atticus drummed his fingers on his desk, considering the question. "You think he was telling the truth when he told you he didn't know anything about a hostage?"

"I do. He looked surprised."

"It may be he didn't want me to know what you two were up to but wants you out of his way. Calling the school board might have been his way of warning you to quit snooping."

"Well, it worked."

Atticus rose. "Good. You are in way over your head. Stay in your lane, Tabitha," he said, not unkindly. "Now for Miss Lancaster."

'Tabitha'? Is he concerned about me?

Libby gave her a wink as they passed in the hall. "I've got this," she whispered. "Meet me at the cafe."

Oh dear.

Up front, Yaeleen waited at her desk, hands behind her head and a big grin on her face. She pointed at Libby's retreating back. "And *she* is your pick for a partner in crime?" Even out on the sidewalk, Tabitha could hear Yaeleen's cackling chasing after her.

·············

In the cafe, Tabitha's cheeks burned as everyone stopped talking and stared—or at least she felt like they were. She'd been warned about being seen in town during school hours; everyone would wonder why she wasn't at work. She sat by the front window so she wouldn't have to make eye contact. It felt like an eternity before Libby sauntered in. She waved to the room, but Tabitha could see that her heart wasn't in it. She plonked down in the booth.

"Did you order yet?"

"No."

"Good. Let's go."

"We can't. Nick's picking us up."

"You called him?"

"How else would we get home? Why'd it take you so long?"

"Well, I'm just sayin'—you could have told me you were gonna tell the truth. Atticus got on to me real bad. Said some mean stuff about stealth-mode, too. Said we better stop, or else. I believe the term 'house arrest' might have been used. And you know the worst part? He said you and me might oughta' stay away from each other. The gall of that boy."

An older waitress Tabitha hadn't seen before asked if they were ready to order. "Yes, but please make it to-go." Nick honked from his truck. "Never mind. Sorry."

·····•·•····

They crowded into the cab, Tabitha in the middle.

"Where to, Miss Libby?" Nick asked.

"Home, I guess. You know what?" She didn't wait for a response. "That Coach Randall is up to no good. We may not have caught him at anything, but something's fishy. And we still don't know who A. Reed is." Nick leaned around Tabitha to look at Libby incredulously. "Oh Nick, don't have a conniption fit. I know—mind our business. I am, don't worry."

Nick settled back in his seat. "Turn here?"

"Yeah." She opened the truck door and eased out. "Thank you for the ride."

"Of course. Any time."

"See ya later, girl. It was fun." Tabitha studied her hands, trying not to smile. Libby leaned in and whispered in her ear, "We still have to find Skye," then ran up the stairs to her apartment as fast as any seventy-eight-year-old could.

"What did she say?"

"Said she still wants to have a girls' night out. Just a movie or something."

Nick studied Tabitha for a long minute, eyes narrowed, then shook his head and put the truck in reverse.

"So what now?"

"Nick, could we stop at the cafe? I haven't eaten."

"Gran left food out, just in case."

"She's the best. Let's go home. I'll practice for a while. Have you eaten?"

"I ate with Gran. I have some work to do at the dojo. Are you okay alone?"

Tabitha scrunched her face up. "Of course. I just told you I'm staying at the house and practicing."

"Do that, please. I would like a calm evening."

·········

It felt good to feel the flute under her fingers. After her warm-up, Tabitha pulled out her favorite book of etudes. Her phone buzzed. She looked at it, irritated at being interrupted.

"What, Libby."

"Don't sound so happy to hear me. We need to talk."

"I'm practicing."

"Can't you take a break?"

"No." *Everyone is always asking me to take a break.* Tabitha looked at her phone. *Three-thirty.* She'd practiced for two hours. Not bad, she could afford a break. "I have no ride. Can you pick me up?"

"The Cadi is in the shop."

"Let's meet halfway, at the Sweet Shoppe."

"Okay. Twenty minutes."

"See you then."

Tabitha swabbed out her flute. *I should not be doing this.* She snapped the case shut, grabbed her jacket, and ran out the door.

••••••••••

Libby, already seated at a table by the window by the time Tabitha arrived, had changed into a neon-green jogging suit, electric-blue sneakers, and a lemon-yellow sweatband encasing her orange curls. She tapped on the glass as soon as she saw Tabitha and pointed to a huge plate of sugar cookies in front of her.

"I see you've ordered," said Tabitha as she unbuttoned her jacket, hanging it on the chair back.

"I always work up an appetite when I run," she explained. "But let's get down to business. A. Reed, or whoever it is, has to be held hostage on the Blackhorn spread. I can pick you up at midnight."

"Are you crazy?" Tabitha practically yelled.

"Lower your voice. We don't want to attract attention."

"The Blackhorn's? Are you crazy? We are *not* going out there. I almost got shot the other day, and you could have killed a man, not to mention we may lose our jobs. And go to jail. Did you not hear a single thing Atticus said?"

Libby flapped her hands like she was shooing flies. "I did. But I've been thinking." She picked up a cookie.

"Well, stop it."

Libby hunched forward and crooked her finger. Tabitha leaned closer, despite herself.

"It's that Ned Ryan." Tabitha opened her mouth to speak, but Libby rushed on. "Now think about it. He knows Coach Randall—we saw them together. He works out at Happy Haze with Bonnie and Vinnie. He has a beef with the Blackhorns. I bet he stashed his hostage out there." She sat back and munched a cookie, proud of herself.

"We're still not getting involved."

"My guess is whoever is the kidnapper is also the murderer. And I bet he knows by now that we're on to him. If I was a bad guy, I'd get rid of whoever is in that cage as fast as I could, whatever it takes."

Tabitha tapped her top lip. "No."

"Could live with yourself if someone dies and you could have helped them but didn't, because you wanted to keep your job?"

Tabitha scrunched her face up, burying it in her hands. "No."

"Meet me behind the laundry mat at midnight?"

Tabitha sighed. "Stealth-mode."

Chapter 25

May Day

Tabitha excused herself from the dinner table early so she could sneak down the outside stairs before Nick turned in for the night. She turned on her reading lamp. Turned the shower on and wet a washcloth, then hung it on the shower rod in the hope that Nick would think she'd already showered and gone to bed.

A few fat snowflakes began falling but didn't stick. Tabitha walked fast, trying to stay warm, and got to the laundromat earlier than planned. The rear parking lot was pitch black, making Tabitha even more nervous She was sure it hadn't been this dark the last time she and Libby met. She shined her phone flashlight around. Broken glass lay under the single street light. *Figures*.

She pulled out her phone. "Libby, where are you?"

"I'm home. Where are you?

"I'm at the laundromat."

"Already? It's not near midnight."

"I had to sneak out before Nick went to bed. Can you come get me?"

"Judge Judy is on."

"*Libby*."

"Fine. I'll be there in five."

·····●·····

The minute they arrived at her apartment, Libby flopped down across a huge lime-green velvet sofa. She looked comfy, like she might not want to get out again.

"Want to call it off?" asked Tabitha, hoping for a yes.

"We can't. You know that. This is good, though. We can make a plan." Libby had a bag of potato chips out and Tabitha helped herself.

"Have you ever been out there? Do you know where these pens are?" Tabitha asked, her mouth full of chips.

"They're in the main barn, but somebody would notice a hostage in the main barn."

"True." Tabitha rummaged through Libby's refrigerator. "Do you have any dip?"

"There should be some green onion in the back."

Tabitha dug around a little longer, then held it up, triumphant.

"Is it still good?"

Tabitha pulled the top off. "Good enough." She grabbed a can of pop from the refrigerator. "So where do you think they might hide a hostage?"

"It's winter, so they're not using their tractors much. If it was me, I might keep a hostage there."

"We need to make some ground rules this time."

"Like what?"

"Like no hitting people in the head with shovels."

"Yeah, that wasn't a good idea. I was improvising. But don't worry, that won't happen again."

"Good."

"Agnes gave me her gun."

Tabitha's chin dropped. "Oh my god, do not bring a gun."

Libby flopped back on the sofa, laughing. "Just kidding. I did buy some pepper spray."

·····•·····

"Do you like Fleetwood Mac?" Libby asked as she put in a CD.

"Who doesn't?" They sang at the top of their lungs the entire half-hour it took to get there. "Why is this road only paved to the Blackhorn place, and not clear out to the Chibitty's?" Tabitha asked between songs.

"Because the Blackhorns only needed it paved to their ranch. I told you they run this town," she said, parking on the gravel shoulder. "This time we're gonna steer clear of the gate and the house. This place has security so we need to go through the field. At least you wore sensible shoes."

Clouds obscured the moon as they sneaked across the field. Libby gestured to a large metal barn. "I think it's that one." She pointed up. "Don't get caught on that camera up there."

"There's a padlock on the barn. How are we going to get in?"

They froze as they heard a truck engine. It crept toward them, the headlights off. The women fell back into the shadows.

"That truck looks familiar," Libby whispered. Whoever it was cut the engine. The door opened and the inside light illuminated Ned Ryan's face before he closed his truck door as quietly as he could. He went straight to the barn door, a small box in one hand and a key in the other, fumbled with the lock, then disappeared inside. He'd pulled the door to but did not latch it behind him. Tabitha tapped her lip, then darted in behind him. Libby waited a beat, then scurried after her like a demented squirrel. She never saw it coming.

Ryan's flashlight shone toward the back of the barn and Tabitha heard shoes scuffing against the concrete floor. She inched closer when she heard the door latch quietly behind her. *Libby.* She sucked in air, waiting for Ned to turn around, but he must not have heard it. She held her breath and listened, but heard nothing more. *Maybe I imagined it.* She waited a long minute before she crept forward, looking for Ned's light again. *What is going on?* It flickered on the far side of a tractor and she inched forward, careful not to make a sound. He lit a lantern. *Thank you, Ned Ryan.* Ned set the box on the floor unlocked a large pen and pushed the box inside with his foot.

"There ya go. Make it last." As he left, Tabitha pressed herself against the wall. When the door shut she breathed a sigh of relief, then heard the fall of footsteps behind her.

"Libby, that was close," she whispered over her shoulder. She never saw it coming, either.

....

Tabitha woke up cold and groggy on the concrete floor. Libby's limp body lay next to her, face down.

"Libby. Oh no, Libby, wake up." Tabitha eased her friend onto her back to make sure she was still alive.

"Ooh. My head." Libby moaned and tried to sit up.

"Stay still," Tabitha instructed. It was still dark in the barn, but morning sunlight now seeped in. "Are you hurt?"

"My pride." She sat up anyway, and Tabitha pulled her against her.

"Good morning," said a female voice in the shadows. Tabitha and Libby both jumped and scrambled away.

"I'm sorry I scared you. The person attached to the voice scooted forward, and Libby shrieked as if she'd seen a ghost. "Don't you come near me," she whispered.

Tabitha squinted in the darkness. The woman looked to be in her early thirties, thin, and in desperate need of a bath.

"You know her?" she asked Libby. Libby nodded, more than a little spooked.

"She's Claire Reed."

"What? That can't be. Claire Reed is dead," said Tabitha.

The woman sucked in her breath. "Claire is dead?"

Libby ignored the question. "If you aren't Claire, who are you?"

"I'm Annette, Claire's twin." She closed her eyes. "Are you sure she's dead?"

Tabitha nodded. "Her body was found a few days ago. I am so sorry."

Annette took several slow, deep breaths, then opened her eyes, putting away her grief for the moment.

"If you aren't Claire, then what are you doing here?" Libby asked.

"I'm an FBI agent."

"*A. Reed*. Of course. You're the one I've been getting the music from. Why me?" Tabitha asked.

Annette's brow puckered for the merest second. "They were meant for Claire. But it's good you figured them out. Who are you two?"

"I'm Tabitha and this is Libby. We teach at the high school. I'm curious; how did you get the music to me?"

"Let's save the questions," she said, all business now. "If you're teachers I assume people will be looking for you, so that's good. We get food twice a day. We have to make a plan before he gets back." Dogs barked and the barn door rattled. "Too late. Libby, lay down and act like you're injured. That might shake him up. Tabitha, pretend you're still groggy."

He came around the corner with a bag of take-out. "You ladies are costing me. You might have to start paying me back." He smirked and winked lasciviously.

Annette held back a shudder. "Look what you've done," she said, pointing to Libby, her gaze steely. "She's injured and needs medical attention."

"She'll be fine. She's just woozy."

"No. She has a head injury. You have to get her to a doctor. If she dies you'll be up on a murder charge. She's old and frail."

Libby, offended at the description, moved to sit up. Tabitha leaned hard on her shoulder and Libby moaned.

He looked at her, uncertain. "Well, I'll be back tonight and we'll see how she is then. Here's your breakfast. He unlocked the pen long enough to toss the bag in. "Enjoy." He sauntered out, laughing. No one moved until they heard his truck drive away.

Annette pulled breakfast burritos out of the bag and handed them out. "He forgot water. Ladies, we're looking at a long day." Annette scooted against the back of the pen. "So start at the beginning and tell me how you two fit into all this. Do you know who the man is?"

"That's Ned Ryan. He works at the Happy Haze, but he used to work here," said Libby.

"Where is 'here'?" Annette wanted to know.

"We're on the Blackhorn ranch."

"As in Sheriff Blackhorn?" Annette pursed her lips, then blew out air. "I did not expect that. Does anyone know you're missing?"

"If they don't already, they will soon. We're both teachers. How did you manage to get a message out?"

"Ryan's teenage son thinks I'm Claire. The kid is in FFA, and Atticus lets him keep his sheep here. Ryan brings him to feed his sheep every morning before school. The boy is supposed to wait in the truck after he takes care of it, but somehow or other he managed to find out I was here. Poor kid's a nervous wreck, but he's too afraid of his father to go to the Sheriff. I told him I was bored and asked for staff paper, and, surprisingly enough, he showed up with some. I talked him into taking my compositions to the band room so his father wouldn't find out, and told him to put them on top of the piano until his dad released me. That was all he was willing to do. The kid is scared to death." They ate their breakfast in silence.

An orange barn cat slunk around the corner, eyeing the leftovers. "He and I are becoming friends," said Annette, teasing him closer with a scrap of egg. "If we're here much longer he may get close enough to pet." She threw the egg to the cat and jutted her chin toward the main house. "Do you think Atticus is in on this?" Her gaze demanded the truth.

"No. Do you?" Tabitha stared at Annette, big-eyed.

Annette sighed. "No. Let's go over this one more time."

After they repeated their story, Tabitha said, "Do you know who hit us?"

"He's never been here before, and I didn't get a good look at him in the darkness. It's always been Ryan. This man was big, much bigger than the regular guy." They sat in silence, gathering their thoughts before Annette continued. "So Ned Ryan is local. I wonder if the other guy is also, or if he was sent in."

"Sent in?" Tabitha asked.

"Someone called in a tip a while ago. It was the break we'd been waiting for. We knew about the interstate fraud but couldn't find the source. Once I got here, it was obvious it wasn't a local operation; someone big was pulling the strings. That's who we're after."

"The mob." Libby's eyes glittered.

"We don't know for sure, but we were getting close. That's when I got captured, and Claire..."

"Was Claire an FBI agent, too?"

"She used to be. We were both musicians in college but got recruited. I love it, but Claire but was always more passionate about music than me. She wanted a quiet life, but now and again they would pull her in for work like this. Working undercover in a small community can be tricky."

"So she got the job to enable you to maneuver more easily," said Tabitha.

"Right."

Libby piped up. "I'm confused. Does Ned think you're Claire or Annette?"

"I'll let you in on as much as I can. Ned Ryan knew there had to be a mole at the pot farm but couldn't figure out who, and it was driving him crazy. The night before Claire was abducted, Bonnie called Vinnie, distraught, and Vinnie called me. Claire had been out to Bonnie's house several times to give her daughter private flute lessons, so Bonnie trusted her. He and I—as Claire—went to Bonnie's to find out what was going on when Ryan showed up. Someone must have tipped him off. Anyway, he was furious that Vinnie had involved

Claire, and things got heated. The next day Bonnie and Claire disappeared. Claire's place was torn apart. There must have been a struggle. I was sure Ryan has something to do with it, so I confronted him—as myself—and convinced him to trade me for Claire and Bonnie. It blew my cover but I didn't care. When I got here, he was holding Claire, but Bonnie wasn't here. I don't know where she is. Anyway, during the trade, Claire attacked him from behind and he shoved her. She fell and hit her head. He told me she was alright." Tears formed and she brushed them away.

"That's horrible," said Tabitha.

"Annette, how did Vinnie tie in?" Libby asked.

"He's quite the character, isn't he?"

"He's dead," Libby said mournfully.

Annette drew a breath, her lips taut. "I didn't know." She exhaled. "Vinnie was my mole at the Happy Haze."

The corner of Libby's mouth twitched. She scrunched up her eyes and dug her fingernails into her palm. A single tear rolled down her cheek.

Oh my god, is she trying not to laugh?

Annette squeezed Libby's hand. "It's hard. I know."

Libby, unable to contain herself any longer, guffawed. "Vinnie the Rat was your *mole*?" Annette looked at Tabitha for an explanation, but Tabitha had already covered her face, trying not to laugh.

It finally dawned on her and Annette grinned, also. "Did you really call him Vinnie *the Rat*?"

Libby slapped her thigh. "It started in high school. He was so little and cute."

"Vinnie was cute?" said Tabitha, trying hard to envision a cute Vinnie.

"Yeah, well, we'll see how cute you are when you wind up in a dryer. Anyway, we didn't know that name would become his destiny. We might have called him Vinnie the Dentist. Or at least Vinnie the Milkman."

"Speaking of names...?" Tabitha looked at Annette.

"My mother played clarinet, and when my parents found out they were having twins, my mother was adamant that we would not have rhyming names. My grandmother's name was Annette, and my mother had always been fond of the name Claire, so while she was in labor, my father said we should name me Annette, and the second child, Claire. My father had a great sense of humor, and referred to us as baby Annette and little Claire. My poor mother didn't realize what he'd done until the birth certificates arrived, and she saw Claire's name first."

"So... Claire and Annette Reed." Tabitha scrunched her face up, trying not to laugh. Annette grinned. "Yeah, my dad's a riot. Try going through music school with those names."

Libby looked from face to face. A slow grin emerging as she caught on. "Clarinet Reed!" she cackled. "Oh boy, that's a good one."

"So, now what?" Tabitha asked after they managed to calm down again.

Libby jumped in. "Well, there's three of us. How about we jump Ned when he comes back?"

Annette smiled and wrinkled her nose. "Jumping grown men is harder than it looks."

"Well, Tabitha here knows martial arts."

Annette perked up. "Are you good?"

"No. I've had one lesson. And we don't know if Ryan will be coming alone or with his accomplice."

"Hey," Libby said, "I'm thirsty."

"Don't think about it," Annette counseled.

"When do we get a bathroom break?"

Annette pointed to a bucket in a corner. "Any time you like."

Libby blinked, her outrage plain. "Oh no I am not. I'm gonna give that Ned Ryan a piece of my mind when he gets back here. I am a lady."

After Libby went to the bathroom, she lay down for a nap, her head in Tabitha's lap.

"It's looking grim, isn't it?" Tabitha asked, her voice low.

"It doesn't look good," Annette replied. "But I've been here quite a while and I'm still alive, so that's a good sign. He could have killed us, but he didn't. Then again, he still may." She noted Tabitha's stricken look and changed tack. "It sounds like you and Libby have managed to do some great detective work. She's a hoot, isn't she?" She smiled. "Tell me about that catsuit again."

Chapter 26
Missing Persons

"Tabitha, we have to go. You are going to be late," Nick yelled from the bottom of the stairs the next morning. He grabbed his jacket from the coat tree and froze as he realized her coat was not there. He bolted up the stairs and pounded on her door, then flung it open. The bed hadn't been slept in.

"Damn it."

"Gran, she's not here. Call Libby," he yelled, taking the stairs three at a time.

"There's no answer."

"Call Atticus. Tell him to meet me at his office."

"Will do. Be safe." The door slammed and the truck roared down the street.

••••••••

"Atticus, I am telling you again—Tabitha is missing. Gran called Libby and she didn't answer her phone. Tabitha has been gone since last night, and I am sure they are together," Nick repeated, jaw clenched.

"You don't know where they are. That doesn't mean they're *missing*, per se. There is protocol that must be met, " Atticus replied.

Nick pounded the desk. "They are. Something happened. We have to find them."

"Maybe they went to breakfast and are at the school as we speak," Atticus yelled down the hall. "Yaeleen, call the school."

A few minutes later, Yaeleen lumbered in. "School says they're absent and didn't call in."

Atticus cursed.

"We have to move now." Nick paced the office.

"What do you suggest?"

Nick stopped short. "I don't know."

Yaeleen spoke up. "Who else might know where they are? Maybe Agnes? Would Tabitha have called her mother?"

"Why are we wasting time? Tabitha is in trouble, and we all know it. She could already be..." Nick said, beyond irritated.

Atticus grabbed his hat. "Yaeleen, make those calls. I'm heading over to Libby's to see if her Cadillac is there."

"I'm coming with you," said Nick, "And don't even say the word 'protocol'."

They rode in silence to Libby's and pulled into the empty parking lot.

Yaeleen called in over the radio.

"Yes?" Atticus said.

"I called Agnes and Tabitha's mother, but neither has heard from either of them."

"Okay."

"There's more. The school just called. Coach Randall is absent, too."

"Thanks, Yaeleen." He looked at Nick, his jaw tight. "Let's go find them."

·••••••••

The barn door slid open, and sunlight spilled in. Tabitha tensed, catching Annette's gaze as she cocked her head as if to say, *this is unusual.* Coach Randall rounded the corner. *Of course*, Tabitha thought.

"Hi, Coach." She glared at him and he averted his eyes.

"Look, I'm sorry. I had no idea this is what he was up to."

"You're talking about Ned?" Tabitha said.

"Yeah," Coach Randall said. "He said he was taking care of everything, but I had no idea he would do something like this."

"Did you put us in here?"

"It's not what it looks like. I followed Ned out here, and when I saw you, I didn't know what Ned might do and I panicked, but I'm getting you out." He glanced at Libby, who lay on the floor, her eyes closed. "Is she okay?"

"How would I know?" Tabitha felt mean. "You hurt her."

"We'll get her to a doctor." He pulled a hacksaw out of a duffle bag to cut the lock off. No one heard the barn door close.

"Hey Randall, catch." Ned threw him a key, then held up a gallon jug of water. "I forgot to give you ladies water this morning. Thought you might be thirsty. Randell, open the pen."

Coach Randall swung the pen door open.

"Now get in."

"What?" Coach turned to find a gun pointed at his chest. "Whoa whoa whoa. What are you doing? We're friends. Partners."

"Partnership just ended. Get in and close the door. I'll be back at dinnertime. You guys are costing me a fortune in food," he sneered. "But not for much longer," he sang as the barn door slid shut behind him.

"I'm so sorry. I never meant for all this to happen." Randall started to cry.

"Oh, shut up. I knew you were behind all of this," said Tabitha.

"But I wasn't. I didn't know what was going on at the Happy Haze until River and Skye came to me. I'm just an investor; I didn't know there was illegal stuff going on until the girls told me. I told Ned right away, figuring he'd want to shut it down, but he got all worked up, so I guess he already knew. Anyway, he started talking crazy, saying he couldn't lose another job and we should shut those girls up, that nobody would miss either of them, and it scared me so I went out to Bonnie's—we were seeing each other—and tried to talk her into taking Skye and leaving town. Told her I'd give her money but she didn't want to go, so I tried to scare her into leaving. It got heated, but it must have worked because the next day she was gone. I thought it was over until Miss Reed, here, went missing." He wiped his eyes. "Miss Reed, I am so sorry you got involved, but I'm glad to see you're alive. I had no idea he'd kidnapped you."

Tabitha cut her eyes to Annette, who looked away but put her finger to her lips. *He doesn't know she's not Claire.*

Coach continued. "I know you were close to River and Skye. I figure they went to you next since I wouldn't help them. And I haven't heard from Bonnie at all, so it didn't make sense that Skye was still in Medicine Creek. And after the poor girl went missing, I was afraid that Ned would do something to River, too. Heck, I remember when she was born." He wiped away a tear. "All I could do was keep warning her to keep her mouth shut."

Tabitha patted his shoulder, feeling sorry for him despite herself. "It is what it is."

"So… now we wait?" he asked.

"To die?" asked Tabitha, any empathy she had for him evaporating.

"Hell no," answered Libby. "Not me. I still say we fight."

"With Ned here, the odds just got a lot better," said Annette. She waggled her eyebrows. "Gather 'round, children, gather 'round."

The moon, shrouded in clouds, lent the night a cold eeriness. The barn door opened and Ned came in, a lantern slung over one arm, and a large plastic bag dangling from the other.

"You get sandwiches tonight. Everyone, go to the end of the pen while I unlock the gate, and I'll give you your dinner."

Tabitha, Coach, and Annette all walked obediently to the back of the pen. "Her, too." He pointed at Libby.

"She can't," said Tabitha. "She's been throwing up and now she won't wake up. She has a concussion. She needs a doctor."

Ned walked inside the pen just enough to nudge her with his boot. "Get up." Libby moaned.

"Don't kick her."

"Oh, I'm not hurting her. She's a tough ol' bird. She'll be fine," Ryan blustered.

He leaned down to set the bag of sandwiches on the floor and Libby kicked him in the gut as hard as she could. Ned grunted and stumbled back. This was Coach Randall's cue to subdue him so Tabitha could grab the key and lock him in the pen—but Randall didn't move.

"*Get him*," Tabitha screamed. Randall looked at her, rooted to the spot, a dark, wet stain running down his pant leg. Annette rushed forward, throwing herself at Ryan but he swatted her away like a fly. She fell hard, her leg making an awful cracking sound.

"*Coach*," Tabitha screamed again. "*Do something!*" Randall managed to take a step toward Ned before his knees gave out and he crumpled to the floor. Ryan laughed and turned his attention to Tabitha.

At that moment Libby yelled, "*Bonsai!*" and jumped on Ned's back, clawing and scratching with everything she had. He reached over his shoulder, grabbed her by the hair, and threw her to the floor. Tabitha watched, horrified, as blood pooled around Libby's head. Ned lunged for her and she managed to avoid his grasp, but now he had her cornered.

"Hey, kitty, kitty. I bet I can make you purr." His arm snaked out and snatched Tabitha by the hair. She clawed at his face, kicking and screaming, but he jerked her to him as she twisted to get away, holding her tight against him with one massive arm. She could smell his stench even with her back to him. He leaned down and whispered, "It's okay. If I can't make you purr, I know I can make you howl."

She felt hot tears on her cheeks as the realization that no one was going to rescue them sank in, and her body sagged. He felt her give up and relaxed his grip. He moved her hair aside and kissed her neck.

"You can be my little pet. I'm gonna be filthy rich. I can give you everything you ever hoped for," he whispered. "Everything you need."

'Everything you need'. Nick said I have everything I need. Tabitha took a breath and stomped on his foot with all her might, then dropped and turned, breaking his hold. *Oh my god, it worked*. He punched her in the face so hard she didn't feel the floor when she hit, but a moment later, pain coursed through her as he fumbled with her clothes, furious.

"So that's how it's gonna be? I'm not playin', now," he hissed, ripping at her shirt.

She kicked her legs and tried to roll over but he had her pinned. He leaned down to kiss her but she turned her face away, struggling desperately to push him off to no avail. She could feel her left eye swelling shut and turned her head toward Libby, who stared back with one unblinking eye. *Is she dead?* Then Tabitha watched Libby's hand snake down to her pocket and bring out her pepper spray. *Spray it, spray it. Why aren't you spraying it? Wait—did you just wink at me?*

Libby mouthed, "*Three, two, one—*" then bellowed "*Blast Off!*" as she sprayed the mace into Ned's eyes. He jumped up, clawing at his face, as Atticus's voice boomed through the barn.

"RYAN!"

Ned turned as Annette swung the shovel. Absorbing the full force of her anger, he crumbled, falling face-first onto Tabitha.

"He never saw it coming! Boy, that was some major stealth-mode, Annette," Libby chortled, holding her bloody head.

Nick grabbed Ryan by the collar and tossed him off. Tabitha tried to sit up but wobbled, dizzy and Nick held her by the shoulders.

"Are you okay?" he asked, searching her face.

"Yeah. Yeah. I am." She leaned into his chest and watched Atticus cuff Ned and lead him away. Two silhouettes stood at the front of the barn, the sun at their backs. Tabitha squinted to see them. "Nick, is that my *mother*?"

"I believe it is."

"*Mom?*"

Tabitha's mother rushed over. "They told us not to get in the way. Oh, my poor baby. My poor baby."

Nick moved aside as Tabitha's mother fussed over her only child. A shadow fell across them both and Tabitha looked up.

"*Michael?*"

"We came as fast as we could."

"Why are you here?"

"Your mother got hold of me immediately after the sheriff's office called, telling us you were missing. We spent the entire afternoon with a terrible woman named Yaeleen and heard the call come in over her radio. We're here to take you home." He smiled. Indulgently.

Tabitha's mother patted her cheek. "We're taking you back where you belong, sweetie."

Tabitha looked around. "Is Zamarri here?"

"No," answered her mother, bewildered. "Why would Zamarri be here?"

"Never mind."

Michael held his hand out. Tabitha hesitated the merest second before allowing him to pull her up.

"We booked a hotel in case we needed to stay overnight. We can swing by wherever you've been staying and get enough for tonight, then pack you up tomorrow." Tabitha blinked, looking from Michael to her mother, then Nick.

"Tabitha, you do not have to go with them," Nick said, eyeing Michael.

She shook her head. "It's okay. I'll see you at home. Will you make sure Libby gets a ride?"

"I will."

Nick watched Michael's car drive away, then squatted beside Libby. "We have to get you to a doctor."

"Oh, I'm okay. You heard him. I'm a tough old bird."

"That you are."

Annette spoke for the first time. "Nick's right. We both need medical treatment."

Nick looked at Annette for a long moment before he spoke. "Atticus called an ambulance. It should be here any minute. Would you like to sit? That leg looks bad."

"That'd be great. Thank you."

Nick helped her onto a stool, trying not to stare. She looked up at him.

"I am so sorry. I know it's like looking at Claire one last time. She told me all about you. She was a very loving person," she said sadly.

"Yes. She was."

"How'd you find us?"

"River found some music at the school and called me. Said it was a clue. I still don't understand how she figured it out, but it narrowed it down to two places. We went to Coach's place. I am sorry we did not come here first."

The ambulance pulled up, sirens blaring. Nick stood at the entrance of the barn to flag them down.

"Which one?" The attendant asked, looking from one woman to the other.

"They both need to be taken care of."

Chapter 27
All Tied Up

Gran sat in a rocker, an unopened book in her lap, as they pulled in. She hurried to hug Tabitha tight against her as soon as she was out of the rental car.

"Let's get you inside and cleaned up," she said. When she pulled away, both their cheeks wet. It took her a minute to recognize the strangers. "You must be Tabitha's mother. Everyone calls me Gran."

"I'm Polly. It's good to meet you," Polly answered, her smile warm.

"Goodness, Tabitha looks just like you. Come in and let me make you a nice cup of tea."

"That would be nice," Tabitha's mother said, already taking to her.

"I'm afraid we don't have time," said Michael.

"Nonsense! I started dinner once Nick told me you were safe. We're having enchiladas. I've made enough for everyone."

"Yum," said Tabitha.

"Tabs is just here to get her things."

"No, Michael. I'm not. I am going upstairs—to my room—where I am going to take a long, hot shower. Then I'm having tea, then I'm eating Gran's famous enchiladas with my mother."

"I don't think that's for the best. Our little Tabby has had a rough day. I'm afraid she's not thinking clearly," he explained to Gran.

"Gran, will you take my mother inside while I shower?" The porch screen banged as Tabitha went inside.

Michael was still in the yard as Nick pulled in. As soon as Nick's feet touched the ground, Michael said, "Good. I want to talk to you," Nick faced him, silent. Michael waited an awkward few seconds before he realized Nick wasn't going to respond. "Yes. Well. I'd like to know just what your relationship is with Tabitha?"

Nick stared at him with flat eyes before going inside, leaving Michael in the yard alone once again.

Tabitha stuck her head out the door. "Dinner's ready, unless you're going to stand out there all night."

"Tab, come out here so we can—" The screen door slammed shut. Michael punched the porch rail before going inside.

"My poor beautiful baby," Polly crooned over and over.

Tabitha touched her eye. "It's a shiner, isn't it? You should see the other guy."

"The other guy is in jail," Polly quipped.

Gran laughed, and Michael looked around, appalled. "I have no idea what any of you could possibly find funny about this. Tabitha's life was in danger. She could have died today."

"Which makes it a very good day," said Nick.

"What?" Michael said, beyond exasperated.

"She could have died today, but she did not. This is a happy day."

Michael snorted. "Is that some kind of Indian wisdom?"

Gran jumped in. "My stars, Michael, it's just regular old wisdom. Nothing special." Tabitha bit her lip, trying not to giggle.

"Nick, you're right. This is a wonderful day," said Polly. "And thank you for taking such good care of our girl, right Michael?"

Gran patted Tabitha's arm. "From what Nick told me, our girl took care of herself." Tabitha beamed, then froze, her eyes wide.

"What is it?" her mother asked, concerned.

"Oh my... *gosh*, Nick, it worked. I stomped, dropped, and turned just like you showed me, and it worked! It was so cool." She touched her eye gingerly. "Now I'm quite interested in lesson two. The one where you avoid getting punched in the face."

Nick laughed. "You might need a few days to recover before lesson two."

Michael couldn't contain himself any longer.

"As usual, Tabitha, you jumped in without thinking and this time it almost killed you, and yeah, we're all happy you didn't die, but your friend is in the hospital because of you, isn't she?" Tabitha set her fork down, stricken. She didn't want anyone to see her hands shaking.

"You never think ahead, do you, Tabby Cat? No. Your mother and I had to drop everything and come rescue you. Again. You need to learn your limits."

Tabitha's breath came in short gulps. Nick stared straight ahead, his jaw tight. Tabitha's mother looked down at her lap. Gran watched Nick.

Nick spoke, his voice low and calm. "You need to learn *your* limits."

"See what I mean? Someone is always coming to your rescue."

"I don't need rescuing," Tabitha whispered.

"What? I didn't hear you," Michael goaded.

Tabitha spoke, her voice louder. "I do not need rescuing. And I am staying here tonight."

"You should leave," Nick said, his voice still low and measured. He stared straight ahead.

"*Rescuing,*" Michael taunted in a sing-song voice. Tabitha wanted to slap the smirk off his face.

"Tabitha does not need rescuing, because your attack is only words. Mine will not be." Nick folded his napkin and placed it on the table. "Delicious as always, Gran. Thank you." He cleared the plates and took them into the kitchen. When he came back he looked at Michael directly. "You are still here."

Polly fussed with her napkin, then pushed her chair back. "Michael and I are just leaving. Thank you, Gran. Dinner was fantastic."

"My pleasure," said Gran warmly.

Gran walked Polly and Michael to the door. Once on the porch, Michael said, "Thank you for dinner. Please inform Tabitha that we'll pick her up tomorrow at eight sharp. After Sheriff Blackhorn talks to her, we'll be off."

"I will give her the message. It's best you go now."

·····•·····

Tabitha watched the river from her window, mulling the day over. *This is a lot. Maybe I should go back home. I am exhausted.* She lay in bed, her face aching from the punch, her head throbbing. She padded into the bathroom for ibuprofen, then looked at the door to Nick's room. She opened it as quietly as she could.

"Nick?"

"Mmm?"

She padded over to his bed. "May I?"

He pulled back the old quilt for her, and she climbed in, instantly comforted, and nestled beside him. "Nick," she whispered.

He turned on his side. "Yes?"

"Do I need rescuing?"

He propped himself up on his elbow and touched her cheek. "No, you do not need rescuing. But you are worth protecting." He pulled her close and inhaled the scent of her hair. "I do love your shampoo. Now go to sleep."

Chapter 28

In A Bow

Tabitha walked into the sheriff's office, shocked to find Skye slouched in an old black office chair chatting away to Yaeleen, with River perched on the edge of the deputy's desk, eating jelly beans from the jar.

"Skye, you're okay!" Tabitha exclaimed.

"Your face is smashed!"

Tabitha touched her swollen eye. "Where have you been? I've been so worried about you."

"The bad guys are gone, so I got to come back into the light," Skye said.

Tabitha took notice of Skye's jeans and pale blue sweater. "You aren't wearing black. Wow," said Tabitha.

"It's temporary. These are River's clothes. Don't get your hopes up."

"Is that Ms. Peterson?" Atticus bellowed from the back room. "Tell her to get back here."

Yaeleen shooed her down the hall. "Get back there, slugger."

· · • • • • · · ·

"Ms. Peterson, I need your statement."

"Gladly."

After she signed everything she needed to, Atticus leaned back in his chair. "Well, that's all done. Things are looking good. Skye is safe, and I spoke with Agnes. The hospital is going to keep Libby one more day for observation, but they think she'll be fine. Ned Ryan is going away for a long time. He was the link to the syndicate and gave us info that incriminates some big fish, and it looks like he was behind the murder—"

"Murder? There were two."

"The best I can figure is that Vinnie's death was an accident. Doc says he died of asphyxiation. I talked to Kelly. She said Vinnie was eating lunch in the cafe that day, and she remembered him getting a phone call about an hour before you were at the laundromat. After he hung up, he started acting odder than usual. I think someone scared him. He panicked, ran into the laundromat, hid in a dryer, and then couldn't get out. I found his cell phone in the dryer. Not sure if it fell out of his pocket or he was trying to call someone, but the last few messages were Ryan threatening him."

"That's horrible."

"It is. Vinnie was a character, but everyone loved him." Neither spoke for a moment, then Atticus cleared his throat and continued. "The feds are claiming jurisdiction, and I can't say I'm sorry. I'm not sure how things are going to play out for Randall at this point. He thought Annette was Claire—that she hadn't been murdered after all—and now the guy is in pieces. I think he got in way over his head, but he's still responsible for his part. The judge may go easy on him since he did try to rescue you all."

Tabitha tapped her finger against her lips. "As much as I despise Ned, I feel sorry for Stormy and her kids. I appreciate you telling me all this, Sheriff."

"Atticus."

She grinned. "Atticus. I think I'll go over to the hospital and see Libby. Good-bye."

"Hang on, there. I hear that you're leaving us and going back with your mother and your ex?"

Tabitha pursed her lips. "It looks that way."

"I get it. Your mother seems nice. But your ex?" Atticus made a face. "What were you thinking?"

"He's always saying I don't think things through. I guess he's right."

She tried to pick up her purse but it was caught around the chair leg.

Atticus jumped up. "Allow me," he said as he moved the chair and handed Tabitha her purse. She was halfway down the hall before he hollered for her again. Laughing, she went back in.

Atticus kicked the door closed with his boot.

"I know this is personal, but what about Nick?"

"What about Nick?"

"I thought you and Nick—"

"Nick and I are not a thing."

Atticus held her eyes a long moment, then held his palm up. "Okay. What about Skye?"

"What about Skye? I'm glad she's safe. I guess she'll go wherever her mother is."

"I'm gonna get real plain with you on two things. First, Skye is a good kid with a mother who left her to fend for herself in a dangerous situation. No one knows where Bonnie is, and Skye needs somebody solid, someone she can count on. I'm gonna tell you, I've seen these kinds of kids, and Skye will not make it without someone to guide her. You could be the one. And second, you are sweet on Nick, and—"

Tabitha felt the heat rush into her cheeks. "I am not sweet on Nick. He just lost someone close to him and needs to heal. And as for Skye, I don't know the slightest thing about parenting a child."

"You're a teacher."

"Not the same thing. At *all*."

Atticus held his hand up. "It seems to me that knowing what you're doing is not a prerequisite in your world. Tabitha, I hope you stay. You're good for the town—just not as a detective." He shrugged. "Just a few things to mull over. Have a good day, Ms. Peterson."

"Wow," said Yaeleen as Tabitha walked by. "You look like he hit you with a Mack truck. What happened?"

"Let's just say he gave me a few things to think about."

"Your mother and husband are waiting for you at the cafe."

"*Ex*-husband. I'm going to the hospital first."

"Suit yourself."

The bell tinkled goodbye as the door closed.

··········

Tabitha poked her head in. "Hey, Libby, are you awake?"

"Yeah. Come in. I've been waiting for you." Libby's head was covered in bandages, orange curls poking out in odd places. "They had to shave part of my head. I'm going to look ridiculous."

"I wouldn't worry about that. You'll find a way to rock it. How are you feeling?" Tabitha pulled a chair up next to the hospital bed.

"I've been better, but then again, I've been worse. How are you holding up? You got a real shiner, there."

"I'm fine. I've got a helluva black eye, but other than that, I'm good."

"The nurse told me the FBI already picked Annette up, so she's long gone. I hate to see her go; we were good together, weren't we?" Libby grinned.

"We were," Tabitha laughed.

"Well, at least I have you."

Tabitha looked out the window. "Yeah…"

"Hey, did Roundtree get ahold of you yet?"

"No. Why?"

"Well, the board decided that, although we 'helped the community', as he put it, they think it best that we resign."

"That sucks." *But it makes my decision easier.*

Tabitha kept her back to Libby. "So what will you do? Retire? Live the good life?"

"I'm thinking we ought to open a detective agency, what with our skills and all. And we already have the catsuits."

Tabitha laughed at the joke. "My mother wants me to go back with her." She turned back toward the bed to see Libby's crestfallen face. "What? Were you serious? Neither of us has any idea what we're doing."

"Nah, I was just joking around. I'm thinking about retiring and moving in with Agnes." Libby made a great show of yawning. "I'm pretty sleepy. Thanks for coming by." She turned her face to the wall and closed her eyes.

Libby made a great show of snoring. Tabitha waited, then left the hospital and walked across the town square to the cafe. *She's old. She deserves to take it easy. Neither of us knows anything about detective stuff. We're teachers. I mean, what is she thinking? Who needs detectives in a small town? The whole idea is ludicrous.*

She looked through the cafe's picture window at Skye sitting across from Michael and her mother.

"Are you ready to go?" Michael asked as she slid into the booth next to Skye.

"No. I'm ready to eat. I'm starving." Michael rolled his eyes.

Polly said, "Skye was just telling us how much she travels. She's about to pull up stakes and go again. Isn't that exciting?"

Tabitha stared straight into Skye's eyes. She'd never noticed how green they were before. "You can't go. You have school."

Skye's brows shot up. "I just turned eighteen. I'm dropping out."

"No, you are not." Skye opened her mouth to retort when River came to take their order.

"River, aren't you two working on a duet for Solo & Ensemble?" River nodded. She looked at Skye, who threw up her hands.

"You can't leave River high and dry. There's no one else half as good."

"What do you care? You're leaving. Your mother told me." Skye crossed her arms and glared.

"I'm not leaving. And neither are you. I still want to know why my scarf smells like Claire's perfume. And where have you been all this time, young lady?"

Skye and River exchanged nervous glances.

Skye took a big breath. "I may have gone to Claire's the night she was kidnapped."

The entire table stopped and stared, mouths agape.

"Did you tell Atticus this?" Tabitha asked.

"I may have forgotten to," Skye mumbled, looking at River for support. River, however, felt an overpowering need to clear the next table over and didn't seem to hear.

"Did you take her body wash?" asked Tabitha.

"The place was ransacked, so I didn't think it would matter. I was scared. I wanted to smell like her." Skye's eyes filled, and Tabitha put her arm around her.

"So... where have you been?" Tabitha could hear River sniffling as she cleaned.

"I hid her." River wiped her eyes with her apron. "There's an old cabin at the top of the hill on the way to the trailer park. I'm sorry, Ms. Peterson, but you don't know how scared we were."

"River, you did great. You both did great. You should be proud of yourselves. Now, no more crying. I mean, what will people think?" Tabitha grinned broadly.

Michael drummed his fingers on the table. "This is sweet, but Tabby, you need to focus. What are you going to do?"

Tabitha perused the menu, then closed it. "River, what kind of pie do you have today?"

"Kelly just pulled a pecan pie out of the oven. It's still hot."

"Sounds delicious. And a cup of coffee, please."

"Do you want ice cream with that?"

"Absolutely."

"Tabs—"

"Before you go on, here's a fun fact. I hate when you call me Tabs. Or Tab. Or Tabby. Always have. My name is Tabitha."

Michael rolled his eyes. "*Tabitha*, do you really need pie and ice cream for breakfast? That's a lot of calories."

"I do. I'll burn them off in Aikido."

Michael sat back in the booth. "Aikido, as in martial arts? You don't exercise."

"I do now. And I eat pie for breakfast. Anything else?" she said, smirking.

"So what are you doing for work since you're fired?" Michael shot back.

"Where did you hear that?" Tabitha looked daggers at him.

Her mother reached across the table and patted her arm. "Darling, Yaeleen told us she heard you were let go. It's nothing to worry about. You're leaving anyway."

"No, I'm not. Skye is coming to live with me." Skye's mouth fell open as River clapped her hands together.

"You have no job."

Skye piped up. "The Sweet Shoppe is for sale."

Michael groaned. "So now you think you can run a business. Oh my god."

"We don't say that here," Tabitha, Skye, and River said in unison.

Tabitha said, "So it's settled. Libby and I will buy the Sweet Shoppe, and maybe we'll open a detective agency. Sweets and Sleuths. Sleuths and Sweets." Skye groaned, and Tabitha grinned at her new charge. "We'll figure it out. Come on, Skye, we have work to do. And River? Put it on my tab."

···········

Dear Reader,

Thank you so much for reading my book. If you'd like to join my street team or stay up-to-date with my new releases, please email me at hi@LucyGlassWrites.com. I'd love to hear from you! And if you enjoyed this book, it would mean a lot if you would leave a brief review. Potential readers depend on comments from people like you to find books they enjoy!

New by Lucy Glass...
Sweet Murder

People are dropping like flies, and Tabitha—proud new owner of the Sweet Shoppe—wonders; was it something they ate?

And she has no idea why a social media star chose Tabitha's grand opening to record her very public breakup, of all places...

And now Miss Lindsay Sweetgrass is home for the summer, and Tabitha can't figure out if she's really as sweet as honey, or just a small-town queen bee...

Tabitha Peterson is settling into her new hometown just fine, even though it doesn't seem fair that the school board voted to suspend her and new bestie, Libby Lancaster—fashionista, septuagenarian, and school librarian—for solving, albeit reluctantly, the biggest crime in Medicine Creek's history.

Now Libby wants to open a detective agency but all Tabitha wants is time to work on her music. A lazy summer selling baked goods sounds perfect—until people start keeling over. And when Doc Hale proclaims it death by poison, things get sticky.

Can Tabitha find the murderer before her business—and customers—end up six feet under?

....

If you like quirky, small-town characters and fun, surprising plot twists, this whodunit may be just what the doctor ordered! Pour a cup of tea, grab a cupcake and enjoy!

Acknowledgements

Here is where I thank the truth-tellers. Not an easy task, but—to me at least—it's the hallmark of a true friend.

First, I must thank my talented cover artist, J.D. Thompson, who not only captured my vision, but cheered me on all the way.

My dear niece, Holly, was brave enough to read my entire first draft and tell me—kindly—where I went wrong. *Thank you.*

And I am fortunate to have friends willing to spend time going through my manuscript to give me valuable feedback. I met my two Susans through music. Serious musicians both, and lovely people through and through. I count myself lucky to share paths.

Made in the USA
Monee, IL
17 February 2025